ALSO BY KAI MARISTED

Out After Dark

Fall

BELONG TO ME

BELONG TO ME

STORIES

KAI MARISTED

RANDOM HOUSE   NEW YORK

All the characters and many of the places appearing in this work of fiction exist solely in the writer's and readers' imagination. No similarity to any person living or dead is intended.

Grateful acknowledgment is made to the following for permission to reprint previously published material:

HAL LEONARD CORPORATION AND COPYRIGHT MANAGEMENT, INC.: Excerpt from "Lookin' for Love" by Wanda Mallette, Bob Morrison, and Patti Ryan. Copyright © 1979, 1980 by Southern Days Music and Temi Combine, Inc. All rights for Southern Days Music are administered by Copyright Management, Inc. All rights for Temi Combine, Inc. are controlled by Music City Music, Inc. and administered by EMI April Music, Inc. International copyright secured. All rights reserved. Used by permission.

OXFORD UNIVERSITY PRESS AND FABER AND FABER LIMITED: Seventeen lines from "The Horses" from *Collected Poems* by Edwin Muir. Copyright © 1960 by Willa Muir. Rights outside of the United States are controlled by Faber and Faber Limited. Reprinted by permission of Oxford University Press and Faber and Faber Limited.

WARNER BROS. PUBLICATIONS: Excerpt from "Don't Fall In Love With Me" by Lacy J. Dalton and Mary McFadden. Copyright © 1985 by EMI Algee Music Corp. All rights reserved. Used by permission of Warner Bros. Publications U. S. Inc., Miami, FL 33014.

Library of Congress Cataloging-in-Publication Data
Maristed, Kai.
    Belong to me: stories/by Kai Maristed.
        p.   cm.
    Contents: Blue horse—How to float—Autofocus—Rain—Switch—The summer sale yearling—The teaser—Barn swallows—If wishes were horses, my love.
    ISBN 0-679-44410-6 (alk. paper)
    I. Title.
PS3563.A6597W47   1998
813'.54—dc21   97-39826

Random House website address: www.randomhouse.com
Printed in the United States of America on acid-free paper

9   8   7   6   5   4   3   2
First Edition
Book design by Caroline Cunningham

To Costya and Nico

. . . And then, that evening
Late in the summer the strange horses came.
We heard a distant tapping on the road,
A deepening drumming; it stopped, went on again
And at the corner changed to hollow thunder.
We saw the heads
Like a wild wave charging and were afraid.
We had sold our horses in our fathers' time
To buy new tractors. Now they were strange to us
As fabulous steeds set on an ancient shield
Or illustrations in a book of knights.
We did not dare go near them. Yet they waited,
Stubborn and shy, as if they had been sent
By an old command to find our whereabouts
And that long-lost archaic companionship.
In the first moment we had never a thought
That they were creatures to be owned and used.

—from "The Horses" by Edwin Muir

ACKNOWLEDGMENTS

My heartfelt thanks belong to Sandy Broyard, Ulf Buchholz, Nicholas Delbanco, Andre Dubus, Bill Goodman, Margot Livesey, Mike Mee, and Sam Vaughan, and to all my family, for their time and generosity and inspiration.

CONTENTS

BLUE HORSE

He would toss the folded newspaper underhand, so it slapped my chin and then slid to my chest, rising up and down, exaggerating my stupid breath. My hands were untied by then for most of the day, but he kept the dog leashes around my ankles, even though my feet were so swollen that getting across to the bathroom I gritted my teeth against the pain. (That *was* why: so the last thing I'd try was to run.) After a minute I would twitch enough to make the paper drop down right next to me. Not to the floor. If it hit the floor . . . There were limits everywhere. He set them and shifted them around in his head like cat's cradles and all my attention went to figuring where the limits stood, from hour to hour. I tried not to touch the newspaper with my hands because . . . Even when he grabbed and rubbed over every other part of my body I kept my hands up limp and free in the air, as if they were paralyzed, clear away from him. I pictured tiny bits of his skin and grease left clinging on the newspaper. He didn't know how my hands were what I kept all to myself. From the low corner of my eye I could read blurry headlines, upside down.

The couch upholstery—yellow, red, brown wool—stuck up in tufts like *salvia*. Plants I used to water in a garden. Like *infernos*. Word I learned from church.

"Read, miss," he would say.

The ceiling was made out of glued beige squares with holes punched in. Spiders lived in those holes. Two squares were gone and strings of others sagged like ships' sails. I pictured the ceiling crashing down on us both. Dust boiling up to heaven, like in history movies of the atom bomb.

I didn't look at him. Almost never. I was twelve in the beginning, skinny and way too tall for my age—he wasn't any taller. But he had muscles, from working out. Fat muscles braided together, veins popped up against the skin in a blue tangle around his chest and arms. Even on the pillowy couch his weight crushed me so even if I meant to scream, no scream would come.

"*Read*, I told you."

I wanted to. The favor he did for me was bringing the newspaper. He knew that. His mouth zipped a smile quick up one side but stayed low on the other, as if a fishhook was snagged. Black eyes. His eyelids drooped slanted, shutting off the white part. He moved stiff and jerky, holding himself like an old guy who sleeps out all night. But he wasn't old. Dad— someone's Dad, anyway, a man to compare to—had silky gray hair. *His* hair was bristly, black with a kind of rust. Shinier hair grew in long licks on down his back. He smelled. Not only from gym sweat: even after a long shower, the stink hung in the bathroom. Hung everywhere. Strongest up close. Smelled like old blood, like crushed animals lying in summer on the road. I couldn't stop myself thinking: maybe he had killed someone already, before. He smelled like infection. Fever. What I wouldn't give to forget his smell.

She—Conchita—told me okay, it's good, you need to forget. That's when I started to remember. Once one memory works loose it's like falling in the dark, you grab out but you can't stop yourself.

So I'd reach for the newspaper. Shaky. I had the shivers there, a lot.

Sometimes I'd try for a bargain. When you're scared for long enough—so scared you keep needing the bathroom even after nothing's left inside—you stop *feeling* it, exactly. I'd tell him, "I'm hungry. I'm *cold*," because by then I guessed he wasn't going to kill me. Not that morning. For a long time all I had to wear was my pink T-shirt with the Garfield cartoon. The shirt was a mess of stains. Nothing below. At night he laid one blanket on me, brown, fuzzy thin waffles. Do you think I cared about how he could always look at me? Do you?

"Let's hear it. Front page," he'd say. Or: "Look in the Metro section." Or later, "Nobody's forgot us. Check out page twenty-eight. So *read*." He wanted a loud, clear, behaved voice.

I really hated the Photo. Where did they *get* that? It shows *Evvie Fenn* in a plaid puff-sleeve dress. Frizzy hair skinned back in barrettes. Pointy chin propped on the back of one wrist, and huge loony eyes. My eyes were never like that and they could have found plenty of pictures where I smile. The Photo looks like the kind of grudge-holding kid who's set on running away, and I used to worry—that the family were secretly talking themselves into thinking that's what happened. I never cried in the daytime. But at night, sometimes, I dreamed I *had* run away. I woke up into blackness with the couch wool slick and wet under my cheek. Hearing his breath bubbles from in the next room.

Later—even with the newspapers days and weeks didn't add up, all I really kept track of was single hours, sounds, where he was or how long till he came back—later, they added the Drawing. Feathery pencil, arty, like someone drew it for a talent contest. The weird wrongness of the Drawing made me mad, like when illustrations don't match a story. You'd think they could *read*.

This artist was expert at bushes. Bushes took up one whole front corner of the picture. Then there's this perfect street—square houses, flat lawns, mailboxes on posts, boys playing ball, dog—which if you look for half a minute isn't any single real street in that town. And also: in real life there was nobody around. It was that deep quiet middle of a July day.

The kid is walking up the center line of the street. Giant step. Goose-step. Long legs, skinny ass in jeans, and the right T-shirt, the right Red Sox hat—you can't tell if it's a boy or a girl except for the title: *Have You Seen Evvie Fenn?* You see her from behind but her head's turned sideways. Her mouth is part open. Permanently. That bothered me: how somebody knew about the singing, on walks. All kinds of stuff. Paul Simon songs. Hymns—*Balm in Gilead*. Bob Marley. That was *private*.

I'd never walk up the line like that. You hug the side, facing traffic, because in the country there are no speed limits *for all intents and purposes*. That's what they told me and I listened. I *did* listen. The family only moved out there from Hartford that same year. Everything was still brand-new: the curvy hilly roads, streams jumping down rock shelves into clear root-beer pools, the air full of birdcalls and sharp sour pollen. At first sight the school looked like a fancy motel—all shimmering windows, in acres of grass.

I read without taking in sense, just trying to keep my voice loud enough and steady. (My bottom was sore, and all down there throbbed like a second heartbeat, hot and cold.) The mind-print of words stayed though. Later I could call them back, with my eyes closed.

My throat was sore, too. After a while raw spots had come up, inside my mouth.

"Quit *swallowing*," he'd say. "What's the matter with you?"

He never did hit me hard, except the first time. "What in *hell* are you afraid of?" he'd ask. He was *fed up* with my attitude. I'd try to think, *what,* and my head filled up with nothing, nothing spreading like snowfall. No answer.

He brought me food: doughnuts, subs, mostly pizza. He didn't have anywhere to cook, only a plug-in coffeepot. If I didn't start in to eat, he fed me. The way he cut pizza, his knife would gouge down right through the paper platter. The rug was all shrunk red splatters, a mess.

There were certain long moments I could tell he wanted to be nice to me, *do* something—if either of us only knew how.

He changed, then. He stared, his eyes let in more light and

the side of his mouth that could smile sagged, open and curved like a question.

———

Conchita said: You didn't have the *freedom* to hate him.

I laughed so hard I choked. String of firecrackers crackling in her face.

———

The newspaper said:

> *Unidentified white/black/Hispanic male observed in the vicinity. Two black females in a white Escort. Hispanic couple, blue pickup, NY plates . . .*
>   *Towns united in search. Helicopters, K-9, comb state forest. Birdwatchers, Millcreek hunt club riders volunteer. Parents' telephone chain, sensitivity training for school bus drivers, crisis counseling in middle school, noted child psychiatrist to speak at town hall, candlelight vigil at First Methodist. Chief of Police Ferling, quote: "Significant leads, too early to discuss."*

That liar.

> *Ferling, quote: "Evvie is a polite somewhat shy girl who because of the timing of her family's move here did not have opportunity to make many friends yet. Evvie's hobby is singing in the church choir. A neighbor describes the Fenns as a 'close-knit community-oriented Christian family, an asset to our town.' Evvie also enjoyed long walks and knew the locality well. We believe she may have voluntarily entered a vehicle—perhaps to help an apparently lost driver. . . ."*

I had heard the engine revving down, behind me. I expected it was about to turn in a driveway but instead it followed, growling like a dog. I never looked around. I held my head up, walking fast. A red truck crawled up alongside, engine popping. That kind of truck boys drive who get a job right out of high school—jacked up on monster tires, loads of chrome lights. Who would ever get in that truck? The door opened. He was leaning off the wheel. "Hey, miss—" I kept walking. I'd had stuff like this happen in the city, but not in the country. Even though nobody else was there I felt sweaty all over. Embarrassed.

I heard the zip of the handbrake. Behind me the motor still running. I started to jog and heard pebbles crunch under my feet and an echo behind. He caught my wrist and swung me around so I crashed up against his other arm. He didn't say anything. It was so crazy I thought maybe he wasn't real, the sun was shining but next minute I'd wake up, queasy from a nightmare, and it would be midnight. But I was fighting, trying to yank free, kicking on his thick legs. We were moving toward the truck. He slapped me. I couldn't see. At the door he shoved hard and I clawed up and in, because it was the direction away from him. Maybe I got the other door open or maybe I started one scream. Maybe him hitting me again was enough or maybe my head slammed against something inside the truck.

When I woke up, everything hurt. It wasn't me anymore, just hundreds of voices screeching inside my body. A light was on. I saw blood smears down my legs, and it was night.

Lack of firsthand witnesses. No trace of struggle. Unprecedented cooperation with the police of all major metropolitan areas as well as the FBI.

Here's where Conchita wants the story to move *on*. Who cares what the newspapers said—five years back—especially when they got it wrong? But the beginning is what I can remember clearest, as if the years just got shuffled like cards, and the first year comes up closest to me. Right next to *now*. In between, a lot that happened kind of slides together. You probably have to stay awhile in one place, for things to matter.

The newspapers mattered. His trick was to get them from all over—New York, Providence, Boston, Philadelphia—but to me that still meant we were in some big city, where he had those choices. And still somewhere in the Northeast.

Or not. From the heat it could have been Texas. Anywhere. But he only brought back the papers that still talked about *Evvie Fenn*.

He wouldn't let me read any other part. The minute I was done he pulled the paper out of my fingers and sliced the *Evvie* columns out with a razor blade he'd jammed partway into an eraser, for safety. He put them into a yellow folder and crammed the rest of the paper in the garbage. He didn't have books. His TV stood on the floor with the plug taped in a thick ball like after an amputation. The TV looked so sleek and new that I figured it was a present. Not that any friends ever came. Only a few times we heard knocks on the door, which had two bolts plus a chain. He scooted over and gagged my mouth with his callousy hand. I thought about what I'd do if someone knocked while he was gone. That never happened.

There was a window above my couch, and one in his bedroom. I hated going in his bedroom where the sweet-sour smell was strongest but while he was gone, I did. Creep-sliding. It took me forever to get *any*where. His window showed almost the exact same outside as mine: a shimmering parking lot for container trucks, *semis*. Sometimes only the head parts were parked; alone they looked humped and helpless, like teddy bears. Behind the lot was a railroad track. Behind that were two huge oil tanks painted pastel stripes. Imagine having to paint anything that big. Behind that—after a while—I began to see ocean, reflected in the sky.

We were three stories up. I don't know what was on the first floor—stores, maybe. Maybe the place where he ate, carried the pizza up from, still hot. Right under us was the gym. Music, hard rock, and weights crashing so my couch shook. Once I asked him what else was on the third floor. "All storage," he said. Then he started laughing, and I almost did too. His laugh was like a runner heaving, trying to catch his breath. I guessed he owned the building.

"I know she is alive. Somewhere. They will find her." Yesterday we interviewed Mrs. Christine Fenn in the kitchen of the family's neat three-bedroom ranch-style home, where she was baking cookies with the two Fenn boys, Arthur Junior (Ayjay) and Grant. (Ayjay plays center on the Junior Varsity Bobcats.) Christine asked me to convey her sincere thanks to all those who have sent letters and cards over the past six weeks. "I hope in time to answer each one individually, but right now we are trying to keep together a normal family life. It's overwhelming to discover that all these strangers are your friends. It's a sign of God's grace. He is watching over Evvie."

As reported, the Evvie Fenn Reward Fund has reached the $22,000 mark. This sum is offered to anyone with information leading to the missing child's whereabouts. Arthur F. Fenn, maintenance supervisor at Lenox Mills and newly appointed deacon of the First Methodist Church, has set up a special desk *and phone in the family's colonial-style living room to coordinate the fund. Arthur states that "God is with Evvie, in her purity and innocence, wherever she is. His will be done. Our faith is strengthened daily by this terrible trial."*

Your reporter was invited to join in the family's evening prayer, reading the Twenty-third Psalm.

There was a picture to that. Five people lined up, with the chalk-bone faces flashbulbs make. Behind them is the dad's leather lounger and behind that the bookcase wall, filled mostly with china figurines, Hummels, breakable things. The older boy has his dad's same slicked-back hairline. The younger boy has his mom's same high square shoulders and noticeable eyebrows. The mom is wearing her white lace-collar blouse and black skirt. One arm is scrunching up her apron behind her, so she has the whole weight of the Bible in her right hand. They all have their own Bibles except for the lady reporter on the end, who is holding Evvie's. The lady reporter is the only one looking at the camera.

————

"Twenty-two thousand," he said. I couldn't tell if he meant it was incredible, or cheap. "Miss Twenty-two *Thousand*." He took away the newspaper, and rubbed between my legs like you'd rub a cat, and then he reached up under the shirt to squeeze my nipples. My breasts were just starting then so my nipples were puffy and sore anyway, but I didn't know that was natural. I thought it was an infection, from what he did.

I dreamed I woke up in a hospital with people touching me all over, saying, "She's paralyzed. She doesn't feel a thing."

Then they gave me a needle that I saw but couldn't feel, to make me sleep.

When I was little I learned about germs. How germs were on everything, swarming and multiplying. Even on a glass fresh from the cupboard. But worst on other people. *Nothing worse than a human bite,* they said. When Grantie was two he snuck up from behind and bit me in the thigh. I cried out—and somebody big whacked him so hard his nose bled. Next day Grantie looked like overnight he'd learned to wink: his eye was swollen to a slit. I carried him around, playing pattycake and singing, feeling awful, because even if I didn't make it happen, in a way I did.

———

Then there were no more papers. No *Evvie Fenn.* He was in a bad mood: he stayed out deep into the night. Sometimes I lay for hours facing the big empty TV, swampy green eye, imagining shows. I imagined Cosby and "I Dream of Jeannie" and Archie Bunker. The characters all mixed together in one endless show. I could hear the canned laughs as if the TV was really on, filling the room.

There was nothing to read except a stack of old magazines. *He. American Male.* I studied the weird pictures. I remembered a birthday party from years ago, where a hired clown twisted blown-up balloons into animal shapes. In the back pages squares were cut out, like he had sent away for stuff.

Later, the dog leashes lay in a tangle by the sofa. One night after my shower he didn't tie me again, I waited but he didn't say a word. He stared through me like he didn't see anyone, or saw something else.

I tried to sass him, to get his sideways smile, to make him *notice*.

Once I told about the guys in the magazines, their brown and pink and purple bodies all shiny like the balloon animals. And he lunged up from his corner, fast, his mouth wrenched down below the bottom teeth. I went sick scared, like in the beginning. But he didn't touch me—instead I heard a grinding noise. He was tearing up the magazines, two, three at a time. His back muscles jumped. Pieces of men—arms, chests, legs— were falling on the floor.

When he went out I worried he would never come back. I would starve there. I stashed cake and oranges under the sofa. I was skinnier than anyone I'd ever seen. My ankles had purplish rings still from the leashes, crisscross dents I rubbed and rubbed till he yelled at me to quit. See-through skin; even when I hardly felt what he did with me, it left bruises, after. Or if I bumped into something. I felt so out of balance, walking.

———

Conchita said: You were a guerrilla, walking in a minefield.

I was *sick,* I thought. But scared if he found out, he—

You went with your instinct! Sweetie, you were a survivor! Survivors learn how to build up walls to protect themselves. But do you still need your wall? Now? Do you need to keep people out who want to help you? It's time to try to—

Shut up. Okay? Don't start, Conchita. I'm fine right here.

Right. In this shelter?

I've got other places.

Look. I'm not in the System, okay? I don't have any clout, I'm just a grad student from San Diego State. I could get paid for this but I'm not. But you're doing what, for money? Hustling? Yes? Jesus, that is simply *so dan*gerous. You kids always think you're immortal—

So how old are you, Conchita?

Twenty-five.

So you know all about immortal. Will you shut up?

———

"Look," he said. "They've went off their rockers. Nobody forgot us. Now they got us a stargazer. Go on. *Read.*"

I was on the floor, in my corner, eating a powdered doughnut. Dry crumbs spilled down on the page. *Disappeared Six Months Ago: Evvie Fenn.* I hadn't seen that picture in a long time. It was like looking at someone you don't like and hearing them say: You girls have so much in common. Go play with her.

> *Police in Berkshire County continue to aggressively pursue any and all leads in the mysterious . . .*

The old, same story. Then came:

> *Igor Pradesh, noted authority on psychic phenomena, has stepped forward to aid the investigation. Pradesh, a past guest at the White House and on Johnny Carson, claims to have received a "vision" of Evvie. He told this reporter: "She is very much alive. I see water—a lake, or the ocean. Moving rocks—or wheels?"*
>
> *Police Chief Ferling stated: "We're sorry this came out at this time. People feel involved so we get a lot of calls, reports. It's liable to raise false hopes. It's tough on the family. But we're listening. Personally, that little girl haunts me. I will not—ever— give Evvie up."*

Pradesh, a soft-spoken bespectacled man of fifty-five, has
stated that any reward he earns will be donated to a charity.

"Go back. Read that whole thing again."

———

Pradesh. Pradesh. You got me out. You brought Evvie Fenn
back into the papers—his wish, turned against him like in every
fairy tale. Once you saw into his red truck: the first one. Once
you saw down to my feet: puffed up and oozing, how they
used to be. You saw the green lacy tattoo of the eagle holding a
snake in its claws, on his left shoulder.

There'd always been sirens but once you started seeing me
and telling, when he heard sirens I saw him shake. He yelled,
"Who wants to read some nigger mumbo-jumbo in the *newspaper*? What is this shit?"

I knew. It was a game. That game where kids say, "warm . . .
freezing cold . . . getting hot. . . ." Only you were always
warm. Just warm. You were never *wrong*. If you'd just once
been wrong he could have laughed you off, he would have
gone downstairs to work out again and come back spitting and
gasping and soaked, trot-dancing to cool down, in his gray
Reeboks and the stained leather wristbands and weightlifter
belt. Back to normal.

He stayed in. In his bedroom he argued with himself, he
threw things, and I lay awake, guessing the argument. My own
heartbeat drove me crazy, muffling up his words.

He came out and kneeled over me, one knee on each side,
and grabbed and twisted his flesh harder than he ever did mine.
"See what's happening? Nothing left. Will you just *look* at this
mess, for Christ sake?"

Then he said, "Who are you staring at. Your crazy eyes make me want to *puke.*" He pushed on me, getting up. "One thing I always promised myself. Never do nothing you can't walk away from. Nothing you end up sitting stuck with and wishing you'd chose different, the rest of your goddamn life."

I showered every day, and cut my bangs with the newspaper scissors, so he'd like me again.

I dreamed too—about you. Brown face with shining glasses, looking down, like God in the Bible classics, from a cloud cavern in the sky. But how could you *find* me? You could only see what I saw. Less—some picces of pictures through your pinhole camera.

But you got me out, Pradesh. And you came closest to killing me—not on purpose but by your game, the *way* you saw. I don't blame you. But these days I almost understand him. I understand fear.

Was that the end? After that night, did you go blind? Or did he lose you after all, *after,* driving away fast, always at night, changing direction with no map? I copied road signs in my head for you, the towns with queer names—*Delhi, Bleecker, Nineveh*—for miles after we'd passed by them. Days.

The next year, did you ever see me, outside the Easy Street Cafe, or Truckstop Trudy's, or the Penalty Box? Waiting, under bushes on the hill above the parking lot, for the customers he sent. Neon below and somebody's boots, crunching up the hill. No hurry. He stood guard and listened, heard me thrash, lying on my back, like making a snow angel, to pull the dry moldy leaves over my face—they were dirty but smelled so clean, like penicillin. They cut through the smell of beer and sweat and mouth on the man. I *wished* you to stay blind. After, he said, why couldn't I do anything right, I was like his curse, his parasite. I rode in the cold wind, in the far back of the truck. Three years we moved around in those towns outside Buffalo, cold blue-shadowed forest towns even in summer, where even little kids didn't cry or laugh and hardly anyone had a job. The men all knew me. My name was Lynn.

———————

You didn't follow us very far. First step, last step. You came so close to seeing all of me, *us*—but they must have decided you were a fake, a liar, after they went out and dug for Evvie where you promised, treasure hunt in the stink under screaming gulls. Only we were gone. Maybe then they simply forgot you, same as they forgot Evvie Fenn. Once they showed your picture next to hers. You're turned sideways with a know-all smile on your big soft lips . . . looking straight at Evvie Fenn.

Can you see me *now*? No goofy eyes, right? Notice how this green eye shadow exactly matches my hair? My hair's this short now, Conchita cut it, she despised the green but I like how it kind of floats over the roots, like moss. This bend in my nose—nothing like Evvie's nose was, right? Conch gave me this earring, she still wears the other one, "until we're together again." Maybe, maybe not. Weepies make me sick. Conchita's dumb trick to make people do what she wants. I wanted both earrings. Silver, and real stones. This one alone drags me down.

I can't smile, because to put on lipstick you stretch your lips big like someone saying *ugh.* The woman behind me who's whispering to her little girl in the pee stall, giving instructions what to do and not sit down or touch anything, looks like she's thinking *ugh,* too. She's watching me do my makeup—like I'm a zoo attraction, like she bought a ticket. In the mirror I have my eye on her, too.

This is a movie theater bathroom. I told the ticket lady I only wanted to look for someone. So I can't stay forever. Smell the popcorn? But you never smelled or felt anything, Pradesh, you just saw. Recently, these last days, I keep thinking about you. And whether sometimes you still can see me. Maybe it's because I'm going back—be there tomorrow if I book it, if I *decide* to—but what gives me the crazy idea you'd be there?

I have to get going. Make some travel money. Only what I really want now is to score, it's a real hunger, like when you've eaten nothing but chips and soda for weeks and you're dying for a healthy meal. I always was able to take the hit or leave it, so why should I need stuff *now*? I don't. I can't. Today's the day before tomorrow. Hey, "Just Say No." At the shelter they gave out a van-load of free T-shirts with the logo and after, in the park, there was this row of skinny backs, in fresh white shirts, drooped over, nodding off. "Just Say No."

It's hot here. *Albany*. In San Diego I forgot how hot the North is, in summer. I grab a paper towel and soak it, brisk swipe under my arms, and in the mirror I catch the woman squinching her eyes like flies are crawling on her face. The little girl flushes the toilet. She's *singing*. I turn around and the woman flattens herself up against the wall. Some guy's tiny wife, candy-floss hair and rouge. I want to slam her. Hard. I see me hitting her, and then taking the kid, still singing.

———

Conchita asked: Are you still afraid? Do you have nightmares? Don't you trust me? How old *are* you? What was your *real* name?

———

That night—was it late fall, Pradesh? Evvie used to know the constellations. If I knew the real date, I'd celebrate, like for a birthday and death day falling together. Light a candle—for not to remember.

I lay on my couch, heard his bedroom door squeal. His step. I was too cold to sleep. I thought his mood had changed and now he wanted to do it with me again. Part of me was almost glad. I was shivering-numb, under the blanket.

The light went on. He threw a roll of clothes at me. Sweatpants, shirt: they had his locked-up rank smell.

"Get dressed." Something was hurting his eyes. They were fiery red. He blinked fast. *"Hurry up."* He went back in his room, and came out wearing a winter jacket, and carrying my old sneakers. "Here. These too."

The clothes felt wonderful. A warm, smooth touch all over.

"Jesus," he said. "What're you, *smiling*—"

"I can't get these sneakers on. My feet must've grown—"

"Hurry *up!*"

I wasn't scared. Not in a usual way. My insides were cold, frozen ripples. I've learned this: the less you can picture to hope for, the less fear you have. I knew something was about to happen, but not what—something enormous, and what I had to do was go with it, the way they tell you to go with an undertow wave, if it ever catches you, at the beach.

He was trying to unbolt the door, one-handed. Swearing. In his other hand the dog leashes threaded through his fingers, and my brown blanket clenched under his arm.

"Shit." Then he looked around the room, but blind, like he was supposed to check for something but couldn't remember what. "That's it. Out. You go first."

———

The air blowing through the street was full of rain, and frost, salt water and seaweed and live earth. I stopped and opened my mouth, simply breathing. The sky was sprinkled with stars, and ghost-bright fish-bone clouds.

"Move." He squeezed my arm hard. I walked, wobbly from the stairs. "*Move* it. You want someone to see us?"

There was no one. Across the street were storefronts, blank windows. No curtains. The street sparkled black and empty, except for a car parked far at the end, and near us, a pickup truck. Older and bigger than the one I remembered.

"Get in. In *back,* damn it."

The bumper was really high. I pulled myself up and hung on, swaying, so dizzy I almost laughed. He pushed me up and over so I fell in, banging the truck drum, noisy, I couldn't help it, then he was beside me and pushing my arms and legs together, tying me with the leashes, and ropes that were already in there, more rope than he needed. "You try to jump," he said, "you'll fracture every bone in your body."

Fracture. He used some words like that. The clouds and stars seemed to be rushing, close, then away, I could feel the distance shift. I asked, "What time is it?"

He was yanking the blanket over me, stuffing it under rope heaps, shutting out the sky. "I'm *driving,*" he whispered. "You jump—I won't hear a damn thing. Don't you think I'm stopping."

Then the truck rocked, and a door shut, and I wondered why he'd dared me. The engine started. The first corner swung me and all the rope coils slithering across the truck bed—ridged and wet and cold—nothing to hold on to.

———

Conchita said: But later—in New York, say—you must have had chances? To jump. To run away.

To where?

Well, *home* . . . But maybe you felt *responsible*? He knew where they were—your family. So you were drawing his power—you were like the maiden in the fairy tale, keeping the monster at bay.

You're kidding.

I want to believe you, that's all!

———

He hated New York State. *Yahoosville. Morons. Welfare cheats.* We were hiding. We lived in a rooming house, a rented Winnebago, sometimes in the truck. I was Lynn and he was Uncle John. He was waiting for some business that never did happen. He made phone calls at night in the snow, he stopped off at post offices and came out empty-handed. Once he took me to a clinic where we said I was eighteen, the doctor wrote me some stuff for an infection, and afterward he chewed John out, loud through the walls of the waiting room where I stood, embarrassed, sore from the exam, hating that doctor.

He planned to go back. Soon, as soon as things worked out. *Home:* his city right on the ocean. He missed jogging in the surf, that built *iron legs.* There were guys who'd kill for his calves, they got *implants,* he said. He drank beers and said: "You too, come on *drink* it; I'm not going to start drinking alone." His grandfather was a tuna fisherman, with his own boat. "You have your people born in their own part of town and dying there, that's thoroughbred. It's mongrels who don't have a clue where they belong."

You made him leave his home, Pradesh, but it wasn't you who kept him away. You were long gone.

The trailer had a black-and-white TV. Only two stations, but he let me watch. "Wheel of Fortune." "Twin Peaks." News shows. Sometimes there were missing-kid bulletins—or kids killed by their friends, or parents—but no *Evvie Fenn.*

We watched a special on deer season, without talking. He cracked his beer can with one hand and spun it into the recycling bag. The bag spilled over—Molson's, Bud, Amstel—all cracked like dolls with little waists. I started to pick them up. He said, "How am I ever supposed to go back? What the fuck do I do with *you?*"

I was quiet. Not remembering that night after riding tied in the pickup truck, but seeing the memory crawl up, like a thunderhead.

"It's not like you can take care of yourself."

"I can take care of myself."

"Nah. Because you're crazy . . . You see how these people *look* at you? If I'd known I was getting saddled with a weirdo—"

"Quit it!"

"See? Bitch. Crazy little bitch, same as—" He came up to me and shoved his belly against me like a big fist. He'd gotten fatter. "Slut. You got the taste for it now, huh?" I felt him move, down below. I hadn't felt that from him for a long time.

He grabbed my jaw. Thumb and finger, like two nails. "So how am I supposed to *trust* you?"

A DAY AT A TIME:
HOW ONE CHRISTIAN FAMILY COPES WITH GRIEF

*Arnold Fenn is a man with a mission. Two and a half years
after the tragic loss of his only daughter Evvie, Arnold has sacrificed the security of executive life in order to host "Jesus Hears
You," a syndicated one-hour call-in radio show. The popular
broadcast recently expanded to three mornings a week. . . .*

It wasn't a real newspaper. Nothing but a Sunday add-in,
floppy cheap paper. The old picture with the Bibles exploded
into grainy dots when you held it near. "Asshole lies," I said.
"Who's *Arnold*? 'Executive life'—what stupid stuff is that?"

He watched me tear it up. He was sitting with his elbows
on wide-spread knees and suddenly he started to laugh, head
flopping down like he couldn't stop himself. I'd never seen him
laugh like that.

———

A letter came. Next day he bought himself Timberline boots
and me a jacket, but he acted furious: whatever money it was
disappointed him. We drove to Indiana, where it was still cold
and no one would talk. Then, I think, Las Vegas. Reno. A lot
of places . . . I could remember better, but there's no reason. I
was always tired. Sometimes he talked us into jobs that we quit
in a week or two before they checked the Social Security.
Working in fast-food places I looked at kids goofing around
and felt like I didn't know how old I was. I wasn't always
Lynn; sometimes he changed to Don, or Frank. In a town outside Sacramento we lived in Hubby's Motor Inn, where there
was a string of taverns up the road, and at night fistfights and

knife fights in the parking lot, police cars turning, and in the morning new trails of broken glass sparkling in the sun like snail tracks.

That's where the second letter came. He waved the ripped-open envelope—thick white paper with a black border all around—and one side of his face kept squeezing up in a smile. He ran out to make a phone call and came back more excited. "Haul ass. Put the stuff in the truck," he said. "I am out of this shit hole. The Lord moves in mysterious ways."

All night, we drove. Highways, twinkling towns, and in the morning I woke up pressed flat like an astronaut in a spaceship crawling straight up to heaven, that's how steep the road was. Fields and scrubby dangling trees slid past, sometimes a shack guarded by skeletons of old cars and trucks. Then there were only trees, tall and thick, ropy branches clattering up the hood of the truck. He switched on the windshield wipers to clear off the leaves.

The house was dusty pink. Inside the chain-link fence, separated by bare ground, were islands of flowers on bushes and vines—purples, reds, yellows—color explosions that made my eyes ache. A good ache. There were orange trees and grapefruit trees, fruit burst open on the dry, cracked ground. Outside the fence locusts racketed in hip-high matted grass, and past lines of hills far away was a dark glow where the sky reflected the ocean. The Pacific Ocean. Right then I thought of you, Pradesh: I wanted you to see me again, in this garden.

He stayed in the truck, head laid on the wheel. Exhausted.

There were live things, everywhere. Quick striped lizards and big white ones. Hummingbirds. Black birds with yellow wings. I stood still, to let them all come back, and then over the slope of the ground I saw something growing, a huge blue animal, blue and shapeless as a cloud, moving closer.

I backed up against the truck.

"That's just the horse," he said. "They told me about him. He's a couple hundred years old. I'm supposed to leave him alone."

————

Conchita said: But who *lived* there?

Nobody. It belonged to some old lady relative of some guy he knew. She was in the hospital. They *invited* him; they worried crooks might break in. . . .

Ha.

Four rooms. Heavy furniture, braid rugs, ivory lace curtains— through them I could see the horse, with his pale blue spots like faded scars, walking on twisted horny hooves between the orange trees. Flat stucco box. California. Nothing like *that* house I can see now across the street—sloped roof, shingles, yew bush at each corner—or maybe it was. All houses are alike. But this street feels like a different country, always dusk, rain falling forever, rain in the gutters, rain in my shoes, it is a different country.

I found my way here northeast—not like it was yesterday, but I don't get lost, I have an excellent sense of direction, I can see places in relationship. Pradesh, follow me. From the bus station up North Main, left over the bridge, past the high school, past the quarry . . . I'm soaked. Shove my tongue between my teeth to stop them chattering. I didn't plan ahead, didn't imagine rain. Whenever the wind kicks, rain falls harder under this tree than out in the open. But I need the shadow.

Otherwise I feel like I'm in bright light and the whole world's looking at me, this street and town and all the angelic host and Conchita—you too, Pradesh. . . .

It's raining. Everyone's deep indoors. Smell the earth? Grantie my brother used to call that "worm smell." See them crawled out on the wet pavement, drowned, like snips of old ribbon? In one house I can see TV flicker, but in this one there's only a single light burning, dim, somewhere deep in the back.

I could cross the street. I could ring the bell.

———

He left, roaring down the mountain. After a while I took a dishpan of water out to the horse and stood back while it drank, sucking and slurping. It raised its head with drops ticking off the muzzle hairs, and stared at me. . . .

When he came back the truck was red with dust. I said, "There's no grass left inside the fence. There's nothing to feed the horse with."

He was unloading boxes of groceries, beer. The horse had drifted out of sight. "It eats the fruit," he said. "Believe it or not, that's a fruit-eating horse."

I lifted a box. I was four inches taller than him and nearly as strong. "Fruit's not enough. It'll *starve*."

But he was right. Later I watched the horse chew oranges off the tree, skins and all, with its stumpy teeth stained brown as a chain smoker's.

He was gone again, for three days. I baked him a cake from a mix in the cupboard. I wandered in and out—showered, then lay out naked on a towel in the sun. I was dreaming of fire, sweat trickling down my sides and in my hair, and when I heard the truck pull up, the gate clank, I didn't move. The cool reach of his shadow opened my eyes. He was undoing his shirt, his stained pants. He bent down. The lick of his breath was hotter than sunlight. Then he was on me, shuddering and pushing in, and I locked my arms around his back, I held on like only his weight could stop me from falling through the hard ground. He grabbed my hands and pinned them back. There were tears mixed with our sweat, his tears splashing down on me off his nose, his face twisted a way I'd seen only once before, as if a sharp deep pain was turning him into something else.

That was the last time he came near me. In the beginning he'd said this house was the break he needed, a chance to get his head together—but then the place disappointed him. It was a dump, he said—it stunk of old lady. He couldn't sit still. I saw how even when he did sit down he tried not to touch anything. I asked how long they'd let us stay and he didn't answer. His swollen eyelids hid the white completely. He wouldn't talk to me. I guessed he was deciding when to leave.

I had my own room. On a polished brown chest of drawers stood framed pictures, babies and wedding couples and soldiers. I matched up their resemblances, gave them names. The drawers below were stuffed with sweaters and nightgowns, satin slips, mothballs. I tried to fold everything back the way I found it.

The bed was high and narrow. Some nights when I lay there, on the quilt under moonlight, the blue horse came. His tarry wrinkled lips, and nostrils, and the nicked rough hair pushed between the window curtains. The globe of a brown eye shone through. But if I lifted my hand he disappeared. He wasn't looking for me.

I had fantastic dreams. I *wanted* to fall asleep, wanted the hot sun-spiked days to rush toward night. I washed all the floors, to watch the water streaks evaporate from the scoured wood like dreams. I pulled down all the dishes to scrub off the oily dust so their picture showed: the ice green weeping willow over a pale green bridge. I went out to look for the horse. When I found the courage to walk right up close it wheeled and cantered away, squealing and gimpy, squirting dust. I took bread out with me. The horse snuffled, snorting in the smell, suspicious, so I had to laugh even though my heart was slamming. I fingered its ropy greasy mane. For a minute I laid my palm on its blue-spotted back, hot as a stone from the sun.

In my dream the nighttime garden was huge, the willow grew tall and wide in the middle, hidden kids playing some game were shaking its branches, the branches' tips floated on a stream, and I rode high on the blue horse, rocking in the warm dip of his back. The horse galloped with big loose strides, and I knew how to ride, I always had, it was soft and easy as flying.

———

Conchita said: Go back. For your own sake. Just to let them see you. See, it's about forgiveness; you could give them that chance, nobody else can!

I couldn't *stay*—

Who says you'd have to?

Long shivers. Jacket soaked, now the rain's over. No nerves in my hands, slap slap, could break a finger. Never cold like this, not since New York. Finished remembering New York. All done . . . Remembering is like eating a path through shit, I told Conch. Joke, okay? Don't look at me like *You march and wash out your filthy mouth. Who taught you talk like that?* Dove soap. Spitting bubbles. They stand so close. *You keep rinsing!* But there is nobody in that house now, where are they?

Light in the front parlor. Light in the hall. *Officer, this is the Fenn residence, somebody out there is watching this house. I expect protection.* I can run. He taught me all kinds of ways of running. Porch light, acid yellow. Door opening, hand, arm, a man, no can't be the dad; this man's all round, stooped, bulgy ass, bald head. . . .

Pradesh?

Oh no *no*. Dog whining—he's letting out a dog. . . .

Rats were what I imagined, what terrified me first—not the idea of dying that night, or the next day, however long it takes to die—but rats, finding their paths through the mountains of garbage and starting in on me, gathering together, more and more, chewing through my skin, face, my insides—oh, I screamed then, not hoping for help, because the garbage barges were tied miles from the city, from anywhere people would live— but so the rats would hear I was alive, and strong, not even near dying. I bucked and twisted under the garbage he'd buried me in, making the rope burn worse, feeling the hot ooze of rope burn on my wrists and legs. I gulped deep breaths in the airspace, sucking in all the poisons and germs. Screaming, deep breathing, then swallowing hard so I wouldn't vomit . . .

Then I had to lie still. I was cut up from sharp edges in the garbage, cans, glass, all invisible things. I kept sliding into a dizziness, forgetting. Listening to my own heart, the way a little kid listens to its music box.

When one first slow long rising whine began, I believed it

was a siren, and in a sudden bursting gladness I thought the
words: saved, savior—I thought it was you, Pradesh—you
able to see where I was, you leading them to find me. . . .
*   I was almost Evvie.*
*   Then another dog howled. And another. I couldn't count*
how many dogs, barking and snarling from all directions, I lay
balled up in the garbage cocoon with my face on my own sour
warm puke and I know I must have cried. . . .

This one's tiny. A toy dog—but it yaps, strutting up on its hind
legs against the leash. The man has a leash that works like a tape
measure, wind out and wind in, and he leans back walking
around the wet lawn as if he and the toy dog were an equal
match. This dog has no instinct. It doesn't see me, but if I
move, it might.

————

In the middle of the night I woke up. Kneeling at the
window—breeze off the hills ballooning the nightgown I'd
picked from the drawer to be mine—I couldn't see the horse,
only clumps of orange trees, waxy black in moonlight.

   I got up, as if it was morning, and opened the door to the
big room. The kitchen area was nearest, all neat, dishes I'd left
stacked to drain—but the lights were on. The lamp behind the
couch was on. That wasn't right. This couch was moleskin
gray, and for a moment, lying curled there in dark clothes with
his back toward me, z-shape, he blended in.

   Four days, he'd been gone. I hadn't heard the truck come
back, or maybe the truck sound was what had waked me. I
went closer. His breath came choppy, uneven, like he was running uphill. His hair had grown out in stringy curls, but there

was a bare circle on the back of his head, freckled orange. He was wearing dirt-caked jeans and a black, sleeveless T-shirt with a sweat stain like a mask between his shoulders. He never let me wash his clothes anymore. He wouldn't sleep in the other bedroom—it gave him nightmares. I hunched down, between his sneakers and the suitcase packed so full it bulged open in a dummy's grin. I thought about having to go away, back to anywhere. *Back.* How that couldn't happen, how to open his eyes, make him understand—

I could smell all the different parts of him. Sugary unwashed feet. Sweaty hair. Used-up beer, and the old fever smell of his body. My arm circled round his waist, and I leaned up to kiss his shoulder, hardly a kiss—only my dry mouth pressed on his tattoo.

He rolled over, gasping. Rising from sleep. I knew that fear spurt, when someone wakes you. I still held him round the middle, my hand jammed down into the couch cushions, and I felt something hard there, a tool maybe, that he'd been lying on.

"What are you trying to do to me? Jesus, what do you *want?*" He pushed away, sliding from under my arm.

"Nothing. I just wondered—if you were okay."

"Shit—"

Then, not caring about what it would be, I pulled the gun free from between the cushions. It was a skeleton gun, skinny barrel, hollow cage for a handle. He'd never had a gun before that I knew of. I rocked back, making a nightgown tent over my lap, holding the gun tight with both hands, careful not to touch near the trigger.

"What is this for?" I thought of the burglars he kept talking about. Then I pictured the horse, walking alone in the night, outside. "What's it *for*?"

His mouth opened and moved slightly but he didn't speak. He just stared. There was a kind of haze over his eyes that didn't reflect any light at all.

"It's mine. Give it. And get out of here."

———

I didn't shoot him.

There is nothing wrong with my memory. I can remember anything I need to. I sat in the room until the windows turned gray, fading out the lamp. Some mornings start with fog, you never get to see the sun rise. He was dead, no need to make sure. There wasn't much blood on his head, but now his eyes shone wide and amazed, letting in all the light there was. They didn't blink. I sat where he couldn't stare at me. I never knew a single sound could hurt that much, it was past sound, like a metal fist slamming your head. It didn't make me deaf, though: after the one shot I heard a drumming, loud then fainter then loud again—the spooked horse, galloping in crazy circles, outside.

When it was daylight, I pulled him off the couch. Dragged him. I knew he'd be heavy. But I hadn't changed out of the nightgown, so once I lifted him it was wrecked, and so was the couch, his blood smeared deep in the cushions, and I felt awful, for what we'd done to the place.

I didn't shoot him. Conchita pretends to believe me, but she doesn't. She *wishes*. Imagining I shot him turns her voice soft and shaky and secret. It's part of why she likes me.

And—I couldn't bury him. It took so long to drag him out

and through the garden to the farthest corner, by the fence. Each time I rested, I looked around for the blue horse that was watching from under its favorite shade, its shaggy sides heaving in and out like it knew what I had in my arms and hated knowing. Orange-eating horse. But then I couldn't bury him. I fetched a shovel but then I only could stand there, remembering, feeling the sun burning through.

I heard the digging. Scrabbling. Fast, steady rhythm. I dug too, faster, deeper into the soft decayed papery garbage, falling deeper, no air left, my lungs sore and cramping to cough, but there was no air to cough with, everything black and whatever my hands met melted away. I wanted to grab something hard, sharp—fight back—where were the things that had cut me?

The air rushed in. Cold touch. Like the cold blind poke of a dog's nose, but it was his hand searching, then twisting into my hair and hauling me up, I saw the first light, thin barred clouds over the swaying ocean. . . .

He said, "I couldn't find you." Cracked whisper like he'd lost his voice. "Every goddamn inch looks the same here." Barges all around us, black mountains anchored in the bay. "I came all the way back to dig you out again and couldn't even find you. . . ."

I hardly knew his face. He was crying. He said it had been his mistake but now he knew what to do, we had to get out, keep moving, go where nobody could ever see us again. He made groaning noises: "uhh, uhh, uhh . . ." He was wiping me down, face, neck, shoulders, with his shirt.

Pradesh? You saw him bury me there in the valley of lost things. Was it after that you lost your sight?

Later you told the reporters wrong, and right. You told them I was dead.

Is that you, marching up the porch stairs, jerking the dog in behind you like a bad-tempered magician, slamming the door? Or was that the Dad? But why is he alone? Where are the others? Whose blocky shadow is behind the lamp and shoving the curtain sideways? Behind the vee of his arm a bright-lit wall of shelves. They're all empty.

When that man moves, I run. Once the door opens again, I'll be gone.

I can't go in. I don't know anymore who lives there.

Flies were settling where his blood had thickened. I never saw a single fly in the garden, before.

I washed myself and dressed, and took what seemed worth keeping, and his hundred and sixty bucks and change, and the gun. I unlocked the gate and backed the truck out. I'd watched him drive enough, but doing it felt powerful and clumsy; I had to concentrate.

There was old rope left in the truck. I climbed out again and went back for the horse. The horse was quivering; ripples ran like water up its legs and chest. But it understood the rope. Once the rope was over its neck the horse walked beside me, stumbling. I led it outside the fence for the first time. In a second the tall, swishing grass powdered its belly with seeds.

When I slid the rope off, the horse stood stiff and high-headed, nostrils widened as if the wind had changed its source.

I tore a fistful of tough grass and held it out. "Here," I said. "Good stuff."

The blue horse took a step closer. Not caring about the

food, though, or about me. It was looking back at the house.
For someone. It gave a sky-splitting, rolling nicker. A last call.

I fumbled behind me, quick, to lock the gate shut.

Then the blue horse dropped the weight of its head, and
gave a drawn-out, soft snort like a sigh, and lipped at some
blades of grass. I stayed as long as I dared, guarding the quiet-
ness there, so it could eat.

How to Float

Finals week. The June day stretched ahead as green and end-less as unfenced prairie. Steve was knifing Marshmallow Fluff onto Cheez-Its, reading yesterday's sports page, when his mother called from work to say the floater was coming.

"Slipped my mind," she said. "There's no money in the house, but he can just leave the bill. Phew. First I remembered you'd get dismissed early. Then I was afraid you'd already dis-appeared somewhere—"

A floater is nearly an outlaw. Only veterinarians can legally work on horses' teeth, but no normal sober vet will stoop to the job. To Steve this degree of shadiness explained why a floater travels alone, expecting an extra hand—an accomplice—wherever he stops.

"Don't worry, Mom. I'm here, aren't I?" Voice bottomed out to bass, a guy she can count on. The Sox had lost their fifth straight. Pitiful collection of crips: bad shoulder, bad wrist, bad knee—the story read like a hospital log. Steve crunched a cracker, a salty sugar bomb. Saliva and greed swamping the undertow of puke urge. His two main girlfriends (more *friends* than the guys were, these girls had the courage to talk, and a drive to dig into the heart of things) were both anorexic. So the girls swore, huddled big-eyed on a bleacher or in a booth, sipping Diet Coke. No one admitted to throwing up, though. Steve wondered: if he were a girl, would he wolf these crackers to the point of stuffed revulsion, and then go heave the mess up till his stomach was wrung empty? He imagined how cleansed and weak he'd feel, after.

"Are you writing this down?" his mother asked.

"What down?"

"Which *horses,* Stevie!" Calling him "Stevie" was how she defused exasperation, how she pulled the rug out from under her own anger. "Which horses need doing. Ray won't remember. Ray's a sweet guy and I *think* a good floater, but he's a little out to lunch. Oh who'm I telling. You were *there,* last time," his mother recalled. "So you know what I mean."

"About . . . Ray?" He didn't want to dwell on it: the last time, down in the barn for an age and a half, alone with Ray. A *too* sweet guy. "Light in the loafers," as Linda Chee would say. Steve had tried to ignore the obvious: that Ray's bright polite interest in him stemmed from the same source as his, Steve's, intense interest in Linda Chee. No big deal, of course. Not the guy's *fault*. But he suddenly wished his mother were home, that she didn't work, that his father still lived with them, even that Francis hadn't died. . . . He mole-fingered around under the newspaper for a pencil stub. "Better run it by me again. Which horses? Duh. You know me."

"Stevie. You fuzz brain! I have to get off the . . . Boss-lady watching. Seriously! Does this *sound* like a business call? Last night all our desks were drug-searched."

"Mom, you're kidding. So *quit*."

She whispered dramatically, "Nobody utters the Q-word." Then she rattled off the horses that were due for floating, and this time he was able to listen, scribbling over the league standings: Gipsy, Thistle, Magick—

"Magick?" A chill washed down his arms, like the sensitivity that precedes a fever.

"Pish tush, Magick'll behave fine. It's warm out, he'll be laid-back; anyway, he's turning into a total puppy if you haven't noticed—"

"He's a two-year-old stud never even been floated before."

"So, he won't anticipate! Use your animal psychology. Steve, I really have to—oh my God, what kind of mother am I! How did the exams go?"

"Fine. It was just French."

" 'Just French.' Just. What are you *eating*?"

"Well, I don't precisely know." He fingered the doughy wad out of his mouth, stared puzzled—a sight gag, but she couldn't see him. The chill returned. "Mom—?"

"I really have to go. You be okay? See you tonight—love ya, babe—"

"Mom?"

"What *is* it?"

"Love ya too."

———

Steve sat on the bottom step. The dog, Harlow, squeezed joy-fully between his jacked-up legs. She was a mongrel bitch with a burden of glamorous platinum fur that had begun its seasonal shed. White cobwebs clung to his jeans, but not where his shiny freckled knees poked through two frayed holes. Steve yanked out weeds that had sprouted through cracks in the wood steps. New maple leaves, across the yard, shimmied belly-up in the breeze like a giant jingled fistful of dimes. Any more wind and the horses would turn skittish. "Spring testos-terone," he heard Francis announce. "Even mares get the hor-mone surge, and geldings too, residual." Steve used to literally grit his teeth when Francis loudly repeated facts nobody wanted to hear in the first place.

Magick, the two-year-old colt, was not gelded.

Uncle Bigmouth. Steve saw no logical reason to respect the dead, and besides Francis was only partly dead. His spirit hung around like a strong smell. Take his truck, for example, standing out there on the patchy grass where it had been towed to, crushed bumper hanging off like a cocked hat. Harlow— *smart girl*—wouldn't walk near the truck. "Maybe you should drive it," his mother had said, hesitant. He had tried that pic-ture for a half-second: wheels. "Nah. *I* don't need it." Part of his job was to protect his mother from what was left around of Francis. Though she'd cried only once, at the funeral, and then mainly from exhaustion. They hadn't decided what to do about the truck, or other things.

Surf sound of cars from the state road, beyond the front field. Suppose someone else drives up—not Ray but the hayman, or a rider friend of his mother's—whom Steve offhandedly cons into leading Magick from the far paddock into the barn. Half the battle won. *Could happen. A lot could. Don't waste your life freaking out.* Harlow's tail whisked his shin.

Ray was late. The sun hung past noon, he'd been sitting here too long, in the vague imprisonment of waiting. Sickish from the junk snack. His duct-taped bio book, for tomorrow's exam, lay closed on the step beside him. To float three horses would take hours. This whole day shot, but he wasn't griping. Because even now that it was down to the two of them she didn't ask much; she did practically all the work so he could make honor roll and still hang out, go to parties, which she never did—though maybe in this Lutheran and Little League town there weren't any parties for people her age. (What age? His mother had a sharp figure, and when she was kidding around and relaxed, her face looked lit up, not just pretty.) Mornings she started the barn chores and nights he could hear her still, washing dishes or laundry, when he reached to shut off his light. She no longer took time to read.

So today she needed him. Period. He could still hear the relief in her voice, on the phone. It pushed his own bad feeling—the weak, trapped feeling—almost completely away.

————

The speculum was a metal and leather contraption with a locked hinge—like a huge skeleton jaw, a toothless shark's jaw. It dangled half-concealed behind the floater's back as Steve led Gipsy into the barn.

"This mare's seventeen. My mom's first horse." Unshod hoofs echoing off old boards.

"We'll do her in her stall," Ray said.

Dazzling sun stretched in a few feet through the open double doors. The rest of the barn aisle was cool blue, the shades of an old movie. Ray himself—sandy blond, trimmer and shorter than Steve, with lines on his face and the perpetual misty smile of a stranger gearing up to pitch something—was washed in blue light. At Ray's feet stood a water-filled bucket from which the steel handles of instruments protruded, and the snake lines of used, translucent piping. The stalls were black holes. Caves.

"Kind of dark in there for you."

Ray laughed gently. "I work by touch. It's light enough."

Steve walked Gipsy into the stall, turned her, began automatically to unsnap the lead shank and then thought better and snugged its chain end over the noseband of the halter, for control. Sometimes the quietest animals can surprise you, and rear up violently in fear, or pain. Steve didn't know where his head was at today. He *did* know, but refused to dwell about it. The weak thrill in his arms still came and went.

"This won't hurt her," Ray assured.

Through the grill bars Steve saw him bend over the bucket, lift one instrument after another, pondering. Didn't he know for sure which to start with? Suddenly Steve saw what else was bothering him: Ray's clothes. The new stonewashed jeans. A white T-shirt plugged down in neat, even pleats, held by a taffy-beige belt that matched narrow, tooled cowboy boots, hardly scuffed. No one dressed like that to work with horses.

Then Ray was in the stall with him, a crisp whiff of aftershave. "Just hold her still for me. That's great. Gee, Steve,

when are you going to stop growing? What are you, six feet?"
He advanced on Gipsy, brought her head down with a deft
twist, not unkind, and slid his fingers into the wrinkly lip
corner to pressure her jaw open.

"Six one."

"I thought so." Pulling out wet chewed grass wads from
the back of Gipsy's gagging tongue. "Wonderful weather so
far. You riding much?"

"Some. Sure." The connection was obvious—the taller
you grow, the fewer horses fit you.

"Showing?"

"Not much. Just keeping these guys exercised." Steve
glanced down at his paddock boots. Frayed laces. Leather burst
at the toe but not noticeably, yet.

"You hunt?"

"Foxhunt? When I was a kid. Not anymore." Glaze of
politeness over his voice, his face, hiding the flash of recall:
hoof thunder, herd panic, fences looming and falling away.
The red-faced men—one was his dad—*half in the bag*. The
shrieking, streaking spotted hounds.

Ray adjusted the speculum over Gipsy's upper and lower
gums, buckling the straps round her head. Now her mouth was
fixed open, wider than a man's upright fist. Her eye rolled
white, in marish apprehension. Steve stroked her neck. "When
I was a kid I hunted on Gipsy. She loved it."

Ray said, "This won't take long. Boy, she sure knows
what's coming, doesn't she?"

Ray ducked through the door to pull a file, long and
heavy, from the bucket. Muscles bunched along the floater's
back and upper arms as he bore down, rasping Gipsy's teeth.
The sound filled the silence awhile, along with Ray's occasional

whistling sigh. Ray's right hand held the cheek piece of the speculum, his left had disappeared almost to the elbow in Gipsy's mouth. Steve drew a cartoon in his mind: tuxedoed lion tamer, head in the wide-stretched jaws. He imagined the force of the snap, the shattering of Ray's arm, if the lock on the speculum ever failed. Now and then Gipsy's knees trembled, and Steve steadied her.

"Sharp molar points," said Ray. "*Shit* load of tartar. She chew her grain at *all?*"

"Eats fine. Easy keeper."

Ray ducked out again for another instrument, a sort of pliers, which he fixed onto a big misshapen lower bicuspid. He twisted and levered, grunting, as if working to pull the whole tooth out. Horses don't have many sounds. They don't moan. Suddenly Ray flew backward, bang against the stall wall, holding high in the pliers what looked like a plastic mold for a tooth: hollow, yellow, and pitted. The tartar shell. When Steve was little he'd collected these castoffs for good luck—the luck was in the sheer weirdness, like finding an owl's crop ball.

"Here." Ray dropped the shell in Steve's hand.

———

Out in the sunshine, Ray drew on a cigarette. There was sweat down his close-shaved cheeks, and confetti-like blood spray on the T-shirt.

"No school today, Steve?"

"It's exams."

"Exams. Brrr. This your last year?"

"Next year will be."

"Wow. And then you graduate." He gazed across open field to the paddocks where horses were grazing; only Magick stood high-headed at the rail, ears pricked. "Gee. This is such a beautiful spot of earth. A real hidden Shangri-la. You must love it. Did you grow up here, Steve? All your life?"

"Yeah. Well." *Mister, what gives you a right?*

With his boot Ray toed the cigarette to shreds. "So. I guess I'm ready for the next one."

Steve shouldered the halter and kicked out through the tangled grass, his heart pumping hard.

———

"Me, I was a city kid." Ray was working on the pony now, all by touch, both his hands probing inside the animal's head while his green eyes roamed over Steve. "East Boston." He laughed. "We played ball on dirt, not grass."

Steve tried to picture the floater as a kid, his own age. Something clicked. "Did you ever work at the track?"

"You guessed it. Reach me that other file. The other one . . . For, three years? Nearly four. Being on the short side, basketball was out, even hockey—my father featured me as a jockey. What else? I wished I'd of used the time for college." The misty smile. His eyes snared Steve's.

"You're not, um, well, you're on the tall side for a jockey. . . ." All this talk about bodies.

"That's what happened. Plus, nowadays, I'd never make weight." Ray removed a hand to slap his gut, which was flat as plywood.

"Did you like it?"

"I *liked* it. I was crazy. I hopped on just about everything. Exercising, breezing . . . They never warn you about what you're getting on, know that?"

Steve laughed a little. "But, you still ride?"

"Nope." Ray stood back. Pinkish drool looped from the pony's gaping mouth. "I can't. I took some hammering. Breaks, nothing serious. I lost my nerve. From one day to the next, I was *scared*." Cheerful, as if the words came easily, no more shame in his voice than if he'd admitted a parking ticket. "It happens."

Steve turned away. There should be some answer. But instead he breathed shallow, seeking fresh air from the stall grill, as if the floater, Ray, had a contagious disease.

He'd felt this same urge for maximum distance around Francis. "You got a problem with me, son? So spit it *out. . . .*" At first, after his pig-eyed walrus uncle moved in, having sacrificed his furnished corner room at the men's residential *hotel* because "you two damn well need a man around here," Steve had decided to see Francis as *funny*. Worked up a Francis routine: grabbing food, belching, flailing a path through his own stinking smoke, even injuring himself—"Damn! When will I learn to slow down!"—whenever a chore needed doing. But it wasn't laziness that made Francis seem not quite human, and not funny. It was his fears. He feared weather, fire, illness. He feared kitchen mice, low-swooping birds, garter snakes. . . . One afternoon, startled awake by the furry touch, he'd sent Harlow flying with a boot to her ribs.

Francis had a lie for every fear situation. Sure, he knew it all, about "equine science"—factoids dredged up from the racing form—but ten paces from a real horse he went into rigor mortis. Then babbled his way out of whatever trap Steve had set. The few times Steve had had to wrestle Magick into the barn—Magick high as a thousand-pound kite, dragging him around in giddy spirals—Francis watched from a safe rise, so

livid with excitement he was already his own ghost. But grinning. "Why don'tcha do it like your mother does, Stevie? You
gotta earn his *respect!*"

There were other times when Steve almost pitied the guy.
Francis had a full-time job, to lug all those fears. And to gnaw
new ways out, constantly, like the rats whose burrows Steve
plugged and poisoned regularly, here in this barn.

"This is a nice type of pony," Ray remarked.

"Thistle? He's . . . after I outgrew him my mother kept
him for lessons. Actually I think he's for sale."

"Hey. *All* horses are for sale. True?"

Steve snorted. *Ours are,* he suddenly realized. Not that it
had been said out loud. But what else? His mother hardly rode
anymore, since she'd had to take the dumb job. And what was
he supposed to do—go on showing greenies that didn't fit him,
no strategy, be a fluke if he happened to *win?* Haul around the
weekend circuit on a shoestring, pretend that nothing was
different? The house was stuffed with scraps from their old
summers together—ribbons and trophies, photos of victory
gallops . . . from only a year or two ago, when he'd still taken
all the glory talk of his "gift" as gospel, as if the single unifying
principle of the universe was riding. With Dad in the back-
ground shade to lend an extra hand, and his wallet, and his monster pride in the two of them: his "winners," the wife and son.

Now the bimbo had hypnotized Dad into an almost
stranger who wrote letters home in chairman-of-the-board
speak. Steve understood that you can't see far into parents'
lives. Not without a diving mask. The bimbo had made her

debut at a horse show, cradled into his dad's arm like the ulti-
mate trophy, but Steve had a sense that in some subterranean
way his mother had moved out first.

The rasping stopped. "I meet a lot of people," Ray said.
He wiped his forehead with the hand that held the file. "I'll
keep this pony in mind."

"Sure." But if they *could* keep this place—would he stay
here forever, tending horses, mucking stalls, riding? Maybe he
didn't pitch in much now, but could she manage without him?
What about college?

Take a year off, before college. Maybe that was what she
wanted him to do—

"This mouth was so-o clean—" Ray said, aiming a turkey
baster, squirting Thistle's raw gums, top and bottom, with
saline solution, "I shouldn't even charge you."

It was a future of pretending that sickened him. That picture. Pretending to stay a kid, acting like happiness couldn't turn
into its opposite. Suddenly he hated all horses, the nightmares,
traps of childhood, drifting across fields and fences and dreams.

Except for this one shaggy pony. He rubbed Thistle's face
bone, where the hard metal of the speculum had dug in.

"Pony's all set," said Ray. "Hello, Steve? Trade him to you
for the next guy—" Suddenly the floater's hand, reeking of dis-
infectant and decay, cupped Steve's jaw and held it. "Steve?
You okay, buddy? Too hot in here? You look a little pale
around the gills."

———

Inside the storage shed was hotter. Sunbaked sauna. Rich
molasses perfume from the stacked feed bags, and wasps hum-

ming against the grimy window. Steve swiped his eyes, to clear a simultaneous spurt of sweat and tears.

Out loud he said, "You *head case*. Get it together." A wind gust slammed the shed door. What had he come in here for? Ray had been leading Thistle away, the fields and fences had wheeled like a Fourth of July sparkler, with Magick the whirligig, leggy center, bucking in the wind. Steve had said, *I'll get some grain. In a bucket. To catch that colt.* There was a bucket in his hand. He touched the scoop that lay on the grain bin.

———

One of Francis's main subjects—but only away from Steve's mother—had been the war. "That's war with a small double-u, sonny. No-name war. Bugs and stink. Shit and dope. Fear you know turns the guts like jelly, whereas dope has a constipating action. Self-medication . . . Dope also smells like peace on earth and slows things down to where you can tell them apart—"

"Steve? What's the holdup, buddy?" Ray calling him now, coming closer, shrill.

The print of Ray's fingers still pressed his face. *What the heck. Ray? I'm not sick.* But what if right now something happened to him—some sudden accident. Ray would volunteer to bring the colt in. No question. Ray was set to buy into the act—any act Steve chose. A short walk, over in minutes. Easy. Nothing worth thinking about. Already half forgotten—

Fifty-pound bags of feed stacked to the roof beam, in tall columns, twelve bags each. Steve reached up and wrenched at the ends of a bag four down from the top. He fell back as the tower toppled, crashing. Dust exploded off the drum of the grain bin; pitchforks, shovels, buckets rattled. Wasps zoomed in a frenzy. He gasped at a sudden punch to his wrist, two, three, hard and hot as grapeshot.

"For God's sake, kid—"

Coughing in the swirling dust, Steve looked around. Would Ray notice how the bin wasn't empty, there'd been no need to haul down fresh grain? Steve struggled to pitch one of the fallen bags, already torn, into the half-filled bin.

———

"Let's see what got you."

Steve uncovered his wrist quickly, before the floater could touch him. "Just a sting." He glanced at the mottled flesh, welts big as quarters. He held that hand inverted and stiff, fingertips curled in, like a claw. "It's no big deal."

Ray bent so close that his breath moistened the cramped hand.

When Steve was little his mother had puffed gently on "owies," to make it all well. Steve shuddered, and he wanted to laugh out loud.

"Nah. There's no stinger," Ray agreed. "Come on, let's go grab your last horse—"

"Yeah, except—" Steve smiled, gritted his teeth, shook his head. Cooled trace of tears. "It's not the sting, Ray. It's my hand. Hurts, I can't move it. . . ."

"Maybe one of those bags landed on it?"

"I don't know. I had this happen once before. Allergy? Took weeks. I couldn't even ride."

Ray lifted the hand and probed between the tendons. Steve let him do it, as if the hand had no external feeling at all. "That hurt, in through here? That?"

Steve smiled. *"Yes,"* he hissed.

"I have an idea what's wrong," said Ray. His thumb slowly stroked Steve's whitened knuckles. "Carpal tunnel syndrome."

"What's that?"

"Hope I'm wrong. But you don't want to take chances. Come on, find me a halter, okay? Let me get your horse."

———

As Ray unlatched the gate Magick shook his mane. Haze deep in the pupils of his eyes. Steve said dismissively, "He's a brat." Under the claw hand, held to his chest as if by an invisible sling, Steve's heart ticked slow and cool. The colt did not intimidate him. He could hardly recall why it ever had.

"Run the chain over his nose?"

Steve shrugged. "Maybe. If you want." He heard his mother say, "It's pure superstition about animals smelling fear, how you *act* is what they have to go by." But his mother was different from normal people, almost like the fear gene was missing in her, so how could she know? Still, to the floater Magick meant nothing. *Was* nothing, probably, compared to all the half-broke rank colts he'd dealt with at the track.

Ray scooped the halter on so quickly that Magick stood stock-still for a minute, surprised. Then Ray gave the chain a testing tug. The colt sank backward in his hocks and Ray went with him, scuttling like a rodeo roper, digging for traction with the heels of his cowboy boots. "Hey, easy there, big guy! I'm not going to hurt you. . . ."

Languidly Steve said, "That's right. Talk to him."

Magick whirled, pranced up beside the floater, snorting.

"Okay! We're fine, Steve, you get that gate now—" Steve worked the gate one-handed and then followed. Ray was doing it right: eyes straight ahead toward his destination, he appeared to ignore the antics of the horse, to anchor himself into the ground with each solid step.

With each step, Steve's hand throbbed. Not his stung wrist, but the hand itself, especially the tendons Ray had probed. It tingled, both painful and increasingly numb. He could almost believe there had been a blow, some injury, when the bags fell. And now—because here in the open Magick was tossing little fake bucks, forcing Ray to stride faster—Steve had to half skip to keep up. But he owned the pain. He'd created it. It didn't own him.

He felt wonderful. Lighthearted. As if all the exams were aced already. He called to Ray, "Funny, how you don't want to ride anymore, but you don't have any problem handling them!"

And Ray called back, words chopped short by the wind, "I guess I like their company! You can understand that!"

"For me," Steve yelled, "it's the opposite! On the ground I can get tense, but I mean, once I'm in that saddle, man, nothing can shake—"

He stopped. Mouth full of wind. Magick was up on his hind legs, towering over the floater, pawing the air. Straight up and about to overbalance backward. Ray played out the lead-line, until he held on only by the rope's tip.

"Ray! Don't hang on! It's not worth it! Let him *go*!"

Ray, low in his rodeo crouch, was sliding in Magick's shadow. Steve edged closer. He was useless—and Ray knew that—with only one hand.

"I'd be spoiling your horse! You want him to learn how to beat you?"

When it happened to Steve, he had let go. The colt had rammed into him, knocked him flat. He had lain on the ground sucking air back into his lungs, seeing nothing but blue sky, until the colt returned to fly over him: forelegs, pale streak up the belly to the full black dangling testicles—he'd felt the steel heat of horseshoes singe his face.

"Whoa, boy . . ." Steve dropped his voice low. Gutteral bass. "Whoa, you Magick." Louder. "Easy. Whoa now. *Stand.*"

Ray had gained on the line. The colt still reared, bobbing.

"Now, get him—grab the halter—" Ray panted.

Steve dodged past the colt's rump. His good hand snatched a hold on the cheek piece. The colt jerked and whipped.

Suddenly Magick came down, four hooves on the ground, his sweaty coat beginning to curl in the wind.

"I have him." Steve's bones soft as water. His right arm still clenched against his chest. Like the Pledge of frigging Allegiance. Keeping up the lie. Wobbly step. He imagined himself falling, slamming the grass. He wished his gimpy hand dared reach out to rub Magick's neck, soothe himself as well.

With the colt between them he couldn't see Ray. Ray whistled as they muscled Magick, like cops marching a prisoner, on the long walk to the barn.

———

"What I love about summer is how the light lasts and lasts."

Sunset pierced every corner of the kitchen. Steve leaned on the counter while his mother chopped stuff. He'd put on a Bonnie Raitt tape because his mother loved tough-girl songs, they brought out her dimple and changed her walk into a hip-swinging stroll.

"You want to talk about life tonight, or just eat in front of the TV?"

Steve flicked his hair back. "You know me."

"Tube." She scattered mushrooms in a pan. Steve turned to look out the window, squinting. The truck was a black hole against the scarlet sky. His uncle's coffin. Find a way to get rid of it. Why couldn't Francis have died of his damn cigarettes, or one of his fears? Driving was one thing the guy actually did well. *It wasn't the crash; it was his heart.* Strapped in beside Francis, ecstatic to be in one piece and goofy from the impact, Steve had cracked some joke that would never be heard. He hadn't realized, yet.

"So . . ." Plates clattered. "Was Ray all right about the money?"

"What? Oh, that character. Sure. We got them done. All three."

"Magick?"

"Got initiated."

"You'll laugh, but I kept thinking about coming home. I really wanted you to be free to study—"

"Hey. Tomorrow's my best subject."

"Honestly?" She took a white enamel pot from the stove and held it toward him. "We're ready. If you could carry this—"

Steve reached with both hands but only one opened and gripped. The pot swung free, crashed on the counter. Shocked, he stared at the steaming lava flow of spaghetti.

"Oh *Stevie,* you klutz—"

His claw was trying to scrabble spaghetti back into the pot. He had to laugh. "Hey, that's weird, I totally forgot, I dinged my hand today. . . ."

"Oh no! *How?*" Up next to him she was so small. She lifted his arm as if it belonged to her. He could smell the garlic and oregano in her hair.

"It's no big deal, Mom. Don't worry, I'm fine." He felt a

sense of awe, as if he were seeing into a mystery too enormous to measure yet. Things that men can do and get away with. Ray the fag knows, Dad sure as hell. Even Francis knew. Now Steve has seen: so many ways to escape. World without consequences.

"What happened? What're all these *marks*?"

Pinkish exclamation points. The swelling already gone down.

"Nothing bad," he decided, and gave her a long, loving look, until her face relaxed.

AUTOFOCUS

Loosen up, they tell me. Surprise is your crucial advantage, and the end dictates the means. Or aren't you convinced of that yet?

But despite my B.S. from Orono I'm no fan of technology. I panfry my bread instead of fixing the toaster grill, and I've stopped using peroxide and depilatories; I'm not a chemical woman. My favorite weapon is a hunting knife my recruiter gave me as a kind of symbol, or a joke. On my answering machine are two buttons whose function still foxes me.

So I was less than thrilled—though I tried to look apprecia-tive—when they showed me the camera. It was a heavy, pro-fessional item, with all those telescoping number-etched rings around the lens that have to be lined up according to some arcane formula in two unknowns. Instead of the usual shutter punch it had one of those arabesque levers that you pull back and release, a system I vaguely recalled from childhood. Some piece, I muttered.

Take it easy, they said. They laughed. (Well, they don't really laugh, but they have a supercilious smile reserved for when they're holding back information, letting someone run in the maze awhile.) Here—you give it a try. Look through the finder. See? In fact, despite the Hasselblad chassis it's com-pletely autofocus. See? Simple? Just center your subject—make sure he's centered, and unobstructed, ha-ha—then pull the—

Trigger!

Lever. And shoot. But not now. Not inside this building, please.

Then they handed me six glossy snapshots of the subject, to study and memorize right there on the spot. You know: a pro-file, three-quarter, one-quarter, full face, and full figure—one suited up, one casual. The casual in this case was a polo uni-form; I remember commenting to them that the helmet cast a bad shadow—this guy would be hard to recognize on the playing field.

Do you know him? they asked. (That's a stock question.)

I took my time, studying. This reassures them. The truth is, I thought I might have seen him once. Maybe socially, when I used to go out socially, before I found my direction. Or more likely in a magazine: his close-ups all had the quality of dreamy airbrushed innocence that you associate with men's underwear models. No, I said. No personal connection. They didn't tell me his name, and I certainly wouldn't have asked. But they told me where to find him.

———

One thing I can count on from them is variety. I had never watched a polo match before.

The gateman was a whiskery granddad in World War I britches and brown bucket boots. He ignored my ID, simply nodded at the camera throned on the passenger seat and pointed me to a parking space up on a grassy hill, with an excellent view of the action. Judging by the other cars pulling in around the field, and by the characters getting out of them, polo deserved its rap as a game for the rich or eccentric: tottery old ladies in blue jeans waved to tottery old ladies in sequined halter tops, teenagers popped champagne corks while their Kennedy-look-alike daddies played touch football with golden retrievers between the Jeeps and Mercedeses. I was kind of wishing for a dog, too, and a picnic of my own, but I was there to work, not enjoy the sport.

The sport was brutal.

While the merely rich camped close to their cars, the eccentrics crawled right down to the rope that divided players from spectators, where clots of sod flew into people's lobster salad and a flying hoof could easily clip someone's face. I followed the example of the eccentrics, kneeling between them, pretending to look for my best shot.

The riders all wore armor, for obvious reasons. Helmets, boots, knee pads, arm braces, back shields—those back shields bothered me; I wondered what they were made of. But the horses wore no armor and that bothered me too, as they came tearing around my corner huffing like trains, eyes swiveling, spurred and strangled by the heavy bits all at once. Mallets swung, missed, smacked the ball with a popgun crack. The horses barged into each other or the mallets or the riders' armored legs; whenever the action wheeled over to my side I'd notice a few lacerations on their hides that weren't there before. Their chests were first stained with sweat, then frothy. The game was played in chukkas, very short innings, because the horses didn't hold up for more than a few minutes of play before they had to be rested, or traded in. But the riders—mostly beefy specimens who dwarfed their scrawny ponies—held up fine. I watched them through my viewer, not intending to shoot but simply because people would expect this of me. The players were grimacing, swearing, having a blast. In all the craziness I had no trouble identifying *him*. He was taller. His armor emphasized the flat-muscled body of an athlete. I thought he rode the best.

I had two maps. One they'd issued to me along with the camera, the other the gateman had offered when I drove in. His was in color, with a season schedule and ads for jewelers, caterers, and tack shops. It showed the parking area, polo field, and at some distance the clubhouse, labeled *rest rooms, phone* (I could see this pseudo-Tudor fortress from where I knelt) and further away, in the opposite direction beyond a sketched grove of trees, the stables.

Behind the stables, on a quiet back road, I had left my second car.

As the last chukka began I got up, scowling and snapping my fingers as if I'd remembered some deadline, and headed for the clubhouse. The camera slapped my ribs. My legs had needle stabs from crouching on the ground. Behind me, the fans moaned at some loss. Out of sight I cut back, into the trees, toward the stable, searching for a certain shape of bend in the winding path. Finally I crunched through brush to settle with my back against an oak, to wait.

Timing would be no problem. I can move *fast:* I train five to eight miles a day, depending. Once anyone got their wits unscrambled enough to find a phone, once the village squad car came screeching through the gate and the crowds, the Oh-my-God-what's-happening et cetera—I would be no part of the local landscape. Gone.

Not everyone is allowed to work alone. But they trust my judgment.

So I saw my best option as shooting him here, from this angle overlooking a good long sweep of the path. From behind. Because otherwise I might have to get involved. Improvise a context, create new opportunities; and I don't like an assignment to drag on forever. Of course I was hoping that the riders would mosey into the woods one by one, more or less randomly after mingling with their picnicking fans and families. Not all in a pack. Because the real issue was *range.* Autofocus or not the damn camera had a short bore; I didn't dare stand more than fifteen feet away.

The grove was all close towering pines except for my one oak. Pines are the gloomiest trees. Every time the spectators cheered I stiffened to attention, expecting the game was over. Then silence returned, except for the hypersonic hum of a deerfly that bit me twice in the cheek. Battling that fanatical bloodsucker I almost forgot what I had come for.

When the first rider drifted toward me, shaking his head and swatting bugs with the helmet he carried, I froze. He was on foot, chatting out loud to the horse he led, a brown and white splotched pinto. I knew them all by their horses now, though no fool would rely on that.

He passed by. After three long minutes the next player appeared. Not mine, either. My mood lightened. This brought the odds of my man coming in last—the best of all worlds—down to one in six.

But he came up fourth. I was ready; I *knew* him, even while he was still partly screened by green branches. A lopey stride, still fresh. His jersey was sweat-drenched. Smiling, he stroked his horse's shiny wet neck. The big, rawboned animal was dancing out leftover nerves. I tested the autofocus, tensed, and sucked a breath. I wasn't here to shoot a horse.

My hand twitched. For a bad moment the man disappeared. Then, through the viewer, I found his eyes: startling, set wide apart. Light gray irises rimmed with black. Eyes like quartz, with their own source of light. He looked straight at me, but that was only a trick of the camera. I shivered from that long glance; his eyes meeting mine, then flickering away again, unaware.

I pressed against the rough oak bark, hearing the beats of my pulse like steps, focusing my camera on the blank space ahead of which he was about to enter.

Then his horse snorted and shied. Laughter boomed from nowhere and suddenly a fifth rider hustled up, yelling obscenities and congratulations on the game. I exhaled as if I'd been gut punched. A question of seconds. As I said, the primary problem was the range.

The blur of bodies—two players now, two horses—rolled on toward my chosen and now meaningless point on the path. I could have used another moment to recover, to erase all the temper from my face—but I stepped forward briskly, like someone taking a shortcut through the woods. Which I was.

"I'll be damned!" cried the rider I didn't give a damn about. (Overfed, bald with Brillo-pad tufts over his ears, and a blood-rich drooping lower lip.) "Have we a delegate of the press? La paparazza, in hot pursuit? Or ambush . . . Oh, my dear girl, *nasty* scratch." I touched my flaming cheek before he could. "Your call, Jamie. Safe to assume she wants *you*."

"Jamie." I never want to know their names.

I pretended girlish indignation. I fluted or whined something about pure coincidence, my lucky day. Why did successful people have to act so suspicious?

Jamie looked skeptical but not unfriendly. Benevolent, like any winner.

"All right, then. Now's your chance," he said. "Close-up?" He threw his hands out from his sides a little, though still holding the reins. Offering himself. That is how I saw him. I held up the heavy camera. It hid my face. Through the auto-focus I saw how filthy he was, and careless—and alive. As if he were on fire, I could almost see through him.

"Now or never." His eyes crinkled in rays, his grin slowed to a secret kiss.

My arm was beginning to tremble.

"I can't," I said. "Hell. I must be out of film."

The other man chuckled. "Haste makes waste, dearie." He reminded me of a dentist, or a priest. "Opportunity never knocks twice."

"Sure it does. Why not?"

I followed them on the path. My only option.

———

I've protected myself, in some ways.

I still know no more than his first name and few personal

idiosyncrasies—he likes thunderstorms and the color marine and the shape of my knees—that don't tell me much and would be worthless to anyone else. While we drove back to the city, to his apartment, I said I was exhausted and closed my eyes. I swear I saw nothing. His mail piles up in a ceramic basket in the hall. I always look the other way, passing. I certainly don't answer his phone.

My camera—*their* camera, really—hangs in his guest closet.

When he notices me watching the clock he smiles and turns it to the wall.

I wear his shirt, half-buttoned, and warm new white socks. The shirt is sweetly starched. We each, for our own good reasons, are careful to keep his blue curtains closed.

They won't be looking for me yet. For some indeterminate time they'll take my silence on faith, on the assumption that I'm following up, working things out, completing the job. Their program downplays idealism in favor of professionalism. And a professional requires trust.

I think of them. What they would think if they knew. What they would do, to him. What they would do to me I can't imagine.

Sometimes I take the camera out of the closet and level it at Jamie. He's so *quick* . . . He's talking on the phone, winking at me, or slouched in his leather chair reading the paper through a pair of small steel-rim glasses that he's fond of because they're ugly. My heart pulls tight when I see him through the finder, the way it did on the day I had just watched him win.

I don't ever want this feeling to end.

I want to open the shutter, stop time.

RAIN

We had a rich Christmas, the kind where you feel the tide pull of redemption under all the razzle-dazzle. I axed a four-foot blue balsam from the woods behind our field. We dippered up Yul glogg at the Svensens' open house (kiddies tolerated), where gold-bangled Birgit Svensen frenched me under the mistletoe. . . . Later, arm in down-padded arm, our whole crowd belted out carols in the moonlit parking lot of St. Ann's. Even Christmas Eve—frantic last-minute wrapping, losing scissors, blackmailing Tara for the umpteenth time back up to bed, arguing beyond endurance about that stupid mistletoe kiss—upheld tradition. Around three A.M. Kate and I sagged against each other, reconciled, smelling of cinnamon stars and whiskey. Wishes, solid and mysterious, spilled from under my lopsided tinsel-tangled tree.

We crept out to crumble Santa's cookies for the jays and trickle his cup of milk into the snow. Tara's miracle, come morning.

The only disturbance I remember from last Christmas—not counting Birgit Svensen's wet dolphin tongue—was a magazine ad I kept noticing: a blank page with the centered quote, *"Daddy, won't you read to me tonight?"* And below: *"Some grown-ups have to make up stories. Support the Campaign Against Adult Illiteracy."* Even though Tara's a big girl of ten, that ad made me want to squeeze her tight and read aloud till midnight. I imagined the man behind the page, webbed in white lies. I sent in my charitable contribution, sorry for any father with a shameful secret to hide.

———

The day after New Year's Carl Ginn summoned me to his office, a glass wedge cantilevered over Boston Harbor. Ginn is the junior partner—the workhorse—after dinosaur Wray and my dad. "Shut door, Russ?" His bald head is round as a soccer ball. He laid his pen like a lock over an open file and arched both eyebrows, the best hair he has. "Russ. I wish to hell there was some easy way to do this."

A prompt for my suggestion. Carl's game is to presume we all know the score, are tuned like walkie-talkies to his plan. I made a show of trying to decipher his file, upside down.

"You've got plenty going for you," said Ginn. "You're young. Compared to some of us." He gave a square, strained grin, like a man with hemorrhoids.

"Thirty-nine." But I grinned back, realizing Ginn knew forty-four, had my records.

"There's no right moment, Russ. I held the troops off till January, figuring the holidays, the tax impact—"

The junior partner is the hatchet man. I remembered—felt, with the same diving squirm—his shoulder pats at the Wray, Turner & Ginn Christmas bash. Then, or even . . . I saw back into last summer, days after Dad had traded in full partnership for a figurehead's low caseload and the mortal bliss of afternoon golf. How at home I had mimicked Carl Ginn's new, bluff friendliness, for Kate.

I said, "You're not dumping me. *Now.* You can't."

"Russ! I sincerely hoped we could handle—"

"You *can't.* You son of a bitch." I stared out at the harbor and when I shifted back toward Ginn blue neon pulsed over my eyes. The same slow-motion panic as fifteen years ago, when I failed the Bar, crammed till my brain was about to explode, and failed again.

"Russ, don't let this be an ego thing. This economy's turned sink or swim—we need wetbacks, merely to survive. Baby grads—*promotables.* Russ—I hear what you're thinking. But don't. Do not go off half-cocked to your dad. Chas Turner isn't—he is not a player now, capito? And by the by—out of sincere consideration for you both, Russ—I haven't mentioned one word to Chas."

His eyebrows begged. Or warned. I pictured my father, in his own leathery office down the hall, chuckling over a joke with the secretary who worshiped him or gabbing the hours away on the phone with elderly unprofitable clients. Lawyer or not, Dad gives out a kind of embracing optimism, as if early on he'd personally shaken the hand of Providence. It's a winking, rosy outlook on life that even a hatchet man hates to destroy.

————

Before our marriage, Kate and I did the independent rebel tango, scrimping in a one-room Back Bay roach heaven. I jobbed for Wray, Turner & Ginn's downtown rivals, rushing contracts around on a twisted three-speed Raleigh. Everyone (Dad and Mother, my two sisters) cold-shouldered Kate. But once we announced our engagement Dad started heavily reminiscing about "the old Turner place," a house on the far side of town where he happened to have been born and which was now by a God-given coincidence for sale. I said *forget* it, this is some sentimental fantasy, no offense. Mother said: But Russell, it's what your father *wants* for you.

To my surprise, Kate had no objections.

And the house, a run-down bungalow lost in conservation land, tugged at me. I can't explain. Pillared veranda. Slate hip roof. Maple floors, chair rails, a root cellar, coal cellar . . . Our windows are the original six-over-six leaded panes, the cleaning woman's nightmare.

Four bedrooms? Kate moaned at first—her happy moan. Dad haw-hawed: you two just fill 'em up with babies! Kate has fluffy brown curls fringing the kind of complexion called porcelain. When she blushes even her forehead turns pink.

Dad cosigned me a mortgage: a token burden. I stacked my textbooks in the smallest bedroom and started work at Wray, Turner. What a bargain, Dad boasted: this boy soaked up law at my breakfast table.

Property and probate. Documentation. I already knew the bins of wills and plot plans, and how to wheedle sour stingy court clerks by their first names. Pretty soon I was handling full cases, over Dad's pro forma. I pulled my oar.

Our house has five acres. I was back in the country, in weather. The day I started clearing I discovered crumbling, silted-over stone walls in the woods. This used to be a *farm,* I told Kate, you wait. . . . I bought a pick and wheelbarrow and worked down there evenings and weekends, slapping mosquitoes and swigging water by the jugful until the last blue summer light. You're getting muscles, Kate said. But isn't this slightly obsessive? I hardly get to *see* you, anyway you'll never—

How do you know? I asked. What do you know, about restoring walls?

––––––––

After my session in Carl Ginn's office I left early. On the highway cars whipped past, honking: what had I done wrong? I was expecting one terrible sharp moment, when the axe would completely sink in. I drove into town, past the "Established 1641" sign, past the golf links and the cemetery and fire station and shops and on toward home, still waiting for the hit.

Our driveway was empty. I walked around the house and down to the woods, skidding here and there in my city shoes as the ground changed from frozen lawn to bulging hummocks under the snow. From between young oaks orange winter sun fanned over my stone walls. I hadn't touched them . . . since before Tara was born. I *had* finished, or at least one Sunday came near enough, after another summer of straining and digging and chinking, to declare a cease-fire: the granite backbone defined a full brambly ghost of meadow out to our land's west edge, where old stones scattered again under a century's debris.

Somewhere near where I was standing now Kate and I had knelt on a blanket, celebrating with a bottle of wine. A windy, warm fall day. When the bottle was empty I slid my folded shirt under her hips and made love to her up against the wall. Her eyes stayed wide open and ineffably blue as the sky above, and I tried to ignore a fear that she was angry or even in pain but then her nails sank into my hips and she came, arched like a high diver, with a huge halting sigh. And then Kate laughed. "Russell? Is it really over?" So I didn't bring up my hope of clearing the meadow, a task I never, after all, began. . . .

Now whips of blackberry sprouted from the wall. Despite thorns tearing my driving gloves I braced and pulled hard but the roots wouldn't give. The leaflessness of winter created an illusion. Though my wall looked freshly built, I was focusing through a blur of burgeoning stems and twigs. Overgrowth.

———

That night we all watched a PG video together. I asked Kate did she want me to shop tomorrow evening, and she said sure but did I have time? And I replied *yes,* and that is the closest I came to telling her what Ginn had said.

If she had been home, to meet me, before I went down to the woods, I might have told her. Who knows.

Next morning I went to the office. Ginn cornered me in the little boys' room. Three months severance, Russ, you can't argue with *that.* And no three-alarm fire, but we *could* use your space. . . . Plus I'm sure you're, er, eager to move on?

I avoided Dad. Left just after he did, at four, and that was my routine all week, and all the next.

Regularly between four-thirty and six I detoured off the highway to a nonneighborhood of body shops and warehouses, and a bar called the Sports Room. Our town is dry.

Over a few Heinekens I read the local paper, every single corny or grisly item, under dim reddish light. By the second week I had a name: "Chief." I picked up some of the other men's names, too: Buddy, Buzz, Jimbo, Slim.

By the time I got home I was dead-tired and only wanted to watch TV.

———

There's something you're not telling me, Kate said.

Kate set the table with little slaps, she kicked doors shut, she burst into tears over a stubbed toe or minor accidental burn. At least you might try communicating with your *daughter,* she said.

Her behavior didn't bother me too much. She simply didn't know she was being protected. In her heavy-breathing silence I was thinking, What if I tell you now, no more tennis at the club? What if I call Foreign Automotive about selling your car? What if we send Tara to public school? And send the cleaning woman back to Roxbury. And you look for something, part-time. . . .

I kept working this list over, back-of-the-mental-envelope, in the Sports Room. But what seemed there like courageous retrenching stuck inside me, sick and cold, when she caught my hand and pressed it against her cheek and whispered: Sorry.

Once I drifted off during the late news and woke up thirsty, believing she'd gone because the only light was the blue-ice glare of the TV. A blanket covered me, my shoes had been slipped off, and for a strange frantic moment, in some lingering dream, I was sure she had left for good. I lurched toward the front hall, still cozy-yellow from the lamp left on for burglars, and paused at the sway of a shadow. Kate. She stood rummaging through the open closet, diving her pointed hand like an arrow into the pockets of my overcoat and suit jackets, pulling up scraps—toll receipts, phone memos— unfolding them with the tiniest rustle, reading, diving in again, with the pure concentration of a fisherman.

I thought, Oh Kate, oh Christ, and backed off. My thighs hit the soft, cushioned sofa. Blind, I covered my face with my hands.

The next evening I detoured out to Lakeview Garden Supply for a half-dozen tight-budded roses.

There's something you're not telling me.

———

I played Megabucks, all the lotteries. My pal Jimbo in the Sports Room explained how the games worked over my protests about what a rip-off, the State giveth welfare checks, the State conneth away. . . . Chief, he grumbled, stop nagging me about the crummy odds. You win, you *win*. Where else can a guy buy a prayer of getting even?

I placed five, ten, twenty-five bets a week.

———

March is my parents' month for Palm Beach. I promised Carl Ginn he'd have my desk early in March. No sooner—I still had cases open. A few.

On the Sunday I'd marked for composing my résumé in privacy, Kate stopped me at the door. "Now where are you going?"

"The office. We're swamped."

"Nothing's that important." Kate stood on the snowy veranda in her robe and slippers, blocking my way, all disbelief. She meant: "no one." "Look at your daughter," she said. "When is the last time you even *looked* at Tara?"

I focused over her shoulder to where Tara was clumsily rolling a chunk of snow back and forth—to build a snowman, I guessed. It was the wrong kind of snow. In her puffy parka Tara looked like an animated snowchild, herself: bubble-shaped, stumpy. We waited eight years for Tara—or she for us, her tiny soul hovering in limbo while I submitted to tests of potency and Kate braved gynecological surgery. The doctor dryly termed our daughter a miracle baby, as if he disapproved of the improbable. "Miracle baby" she was: a near-silent cherub with a limpid smile, and if lavish expectations can create a gifted child our daughter should be one. But Tara today is what her teachers term "a little slow." Is she? Not slow enough, they assure us, to be "exceptional."

Where are her friends, this winter?

An only child. A single child. It took us longer to make this daughter than for me to rebuild the stone wall. Aware of our attention she began rolling the snow chunk faster. When it broke she flailed at the pieces, clowning. "What *about* Tara?" I asked.

"Are you blind? She's been acting extremely . . . withdrawn." Kate squinted up at me. In the shadowless light her face was covered with uncountable frown lines, squint lines, long pocks beside her mouth and chin, all like some sudden, temporary affliction. "I mean, between the two of you I'm nearly—"

"Did you ask her what's *wrong*?"

" 'She wants a pony.' " Kate spoke in quotes. Her mouth twisted.

"Oh, that."

The Christmas wish. How many ten-year-olds still write to Santa? I'd humored her, suspecting Tara of trying to manipulate us—happy to think she was *capable* of manipulating. But I had tried, gently, to deflect her from the pony.

"She can't even *ride*. A pony can be dangerous, we'd need a grass pasture, a barn, we'd need—" Suddenly I had a vision of a new Tara, slender and graceful, cantering up a hill. "Do lessons cost the moon?"

"Lessons? Frankly I don't think it's even the pony she wants."

"Well, good!"

"I think the pony is just a . . . projection. It's *you,* Russell. She—"

"Okay. *I'll* ask Tara if she wants lessons." I reached out for Kate, but at that moment Tara waved. I waved back like crazy, and swung up my briefcase, to show I had to leave.

———

In high school "fun" meant keg parties. I wasn't often invited, not I think because people disliked me but because I wasn't in any crowd, not even the crowd of leftovers who stuck together for consolation, secretly hoping for a ticket out, some success, or a Cinderella romance. When I *was* invited I got drunk fast to show I meant business, belonged. I'd feel myself growing taller, as if my neck was rubber. When I moved the room spun like a tilted cube and I'd hear my own loud laughter at someone's jokes; I'd ask girls to dance, girls I didn't dare speak to in school, and they would nod seriously and stand in front of me, shimmying their hips. When the urge to be sick took over I'd join the guys out on some back deck who were barfing over the rail into somebody's parents' rock garden. We'd catch each other's eye, spit, and flash accomplice grins.

That brotherhood was the point of it all, to me.

And that rush—a whirling loss of balance and inhibitions—was my definition of drunk. Not the white-knuckle, crawl-tempo drive from the Sports Room home. Not Kate's voice grating in my ears, static from an untuned radio. Not my raging thirst during and after a tasteless dinner, because all those beers stayed down, after all, without even taking the edge off the bloated panic that descended at night, pressing and expanding while I lay panting, dog-still, in the dark.

———

Before my interview I got a haircut that made me look like Mickey Rooney. The headhuntress had never heard of Wray, Turner & Ginn.

"You're in a rather special category, Mr. Turner," she fluted. "Marketing-wise. Salary-wise." She was younger than I wanted her to be and tapped a gold Mont Blanc on her snowy teeth. "Special" disturbed me. I thought of Tara.

"I'm pretty flexible. In fact, I view my situation as an opportunity to make a change."

"Right." She scratched a word and smiled. "But we are talking an *aggressive* effort here, Mr. Turner. Our policy for this type of effort is a five-hundred-dollar deposit. Tax deductible, naturally. We urge clients to think of this as an investment in their most important asset. Themselves."

"Well . . ." I felt a sweat break out.

"Up to you. We can certainly keep you on file. For no charge." Tap, tap, tap.

————

How many law firms in Boston? I mailed my résumés, a flock of white pigeons. Most vanished. A few prompted invitations and keyed-up anticipation, until I appeared with buffed nails and college tie to "explore a possible fit." All firms were "lean-and-hungry," their starting packages "an insult to your experience. . . ." The colleagues examined me. I tried to improvise answers, thrown back to my agony of defeat, facing the Bar.

On beer doilies that shredded under pressure I drew the diamond outline of our land. The house's footprint. I sketched in a short access road. Area equals one-half perimeter squared. I was remembering geometry.

Jimbo bumped my elbow. "Subdivision? Boom's over, Chief. Tell your people they'd be nuts to sell now."

I gulped from my glass. Beer warm and salty as a mouthful of sea. In the Sports Room I was a swimmer. "It's my own place, actually," I said.

"No kidding. Big!"

"I'm only considering doing one lot."

"Do one, do 'em all. Who wants to live with a herd of backhoes? Go for it, Chief. You sell, *sell.* Take the loot, head south. All or nothing."

"Yeah. Maybe." I shaded the access road.

Only in the Sports Room could my tongue and lips move to form that word: sell. Stabbing my pen into the napkin, figuring cost and margin, and a profit with a tail of zeros sleek as the Megabucks jackpot posted over the bar. I dreamed southward: to Mexico, or Provence. I saw Kate exploring the native market. Tara, tanned and bold, babbled in a new-found language.

But when I stepped outside the cold, magnified by alcohol, numbed my lips, and my head rang with incoherent reminders about all I had meant to do that day and for no reason had again not done. Driving into our town, stopping for milk, hearing the crash of bells from the Methodist steeple, I felt the air flow warmer. A century ago towns like this had tarred and feathered and banished whoever broke the order. . . . I imagined exile, the slow bankruptcy of memory. I lingered in the convenience store, where the man we all just know as "the Greek" asked: Everything okay, Mr. Turner? I get you a glass of water, a chair to sit down?

Swerving up the driveway my headlights scanned ice- and snow-weighted shrubbery, sap-filled gashes where branches had snapped off. No January thaw and none in the wind yet for February, either . . .

I hit the brakes so hard the car skewed sideways. I leaned forward to rub the suddenly steamy windshield, confused, shaky from the bad stop, and not certain that what I saw was real.

A monstrous yellow object floated in my headlights. A giant raft. The Kon-Tiki, or Noah's Ark: long planks, timbers, strapped and banded.

Eventually I walked around the raft, touched it, smelled the promise and pungency of fresh-cut wood.

I found Kate in the kitchen holding a screwdriver pointed toward me.

"What in the name of God?" I asked.

"I got this for your parents. Saturday's their anniversary. Please don't say you forgot."

She poked the screwdriver into the brass base of a hideous lamp. I grabbed it away. "Listen, Kate, I came *that* close to smashing into a pile of—I want to know what in hell you think you're up to."

"Oh. You want to know what *I'm* up to?" She spoke peaceably, with a queer mousy smile. Then she screamed, "It's for the new *addition,* don't you even remember *that*? We decided *ages* ago, you saw the blueprints! And we agreed to wait until Gerry Dupree could do the work, you even said—"

I went outside and stood looking at the lumber pile again, thinking it was good wood, gorgeous wood, and couldn't Gerry or whoever have at least thrown a tarp over it, in case of more snow? From upstairs I heard Tara's radio playing, only the deep bass throb. I still didn't remember.

————

My parents' house is not where I grew up. They've moved four times, keeping lockstep pace with the town's rising real estate values. While Pilgrim Crescent was under construction the raw airy frames looked so immense people wondered if the developer was trying to put condos over on us. Now brick-front Federal alternates with Tudor alternates with Cape Ann, and so on. Dad and Mother are the Tudor. I'm still not convinced.

Having spent the whole day avoiding a single drink, doing every obsessive thing to occupy my hands, I wondered why my parents' flagstone steps drifted away beneath me, why I still felt drunk. (Now I know drunk has as many forms as a genie, and you don't always need the bottle.) I lugged the pricey brass lamp. My mother took it in her arms before bending for Kate's kiss, then Tara's; she is a tall strong woman, though usually she feigns a delicate incompetence, part of her generation's ideal. "Russell," she said, "how perfect. I *love* it. . . . Look, Dad! Kate always *knows*." As we filed into the great room (mute furniture islands, "conversation groups") I noticed for the first time many pot-bellied table lamps, cousins to ours.

Dad passed whiskey sours, his drink, and shook me by the neck. "How's every little thing, boyo?"

"Fine."

Kate frowned at Tara who was sifting through a silver platter full of cashews. "Don't, darling. Those are the *worst,* for making you fat."

Mother tossed her head back to stare alertly at the ceiling. Forty years dropped away from her stretched profile. I glimpsed the village belle. "I hear her," Mother announced. "Don't you? She *promised* tonight she'd come down."

"Rhoda's going to join us?" Kate caught my eye.

"The clan gathers," exulted Dad. "You kids, Rhoda—and now even Rachel's driving up tonight! Who could ask for more?"

Rhoda and Rachel. My two little sisters. My two screwed-up little sisters, as Kate would say . . . has often said. My two screwed-up, highly intelligent, self-absorbed little sisters. My two screwed-up, unforgiving, deeply deceitful, sarcastic, love-less, aging . . .

I was twelve when Rhoda was born. Rache came a year later. I thought those two skinny dark-haired babies were the end of loneliness; anyway I tried to cuddle them, care for them, even carry them one on each khakied hip, the way I'd seen women do. But they cried day and night, then they were sick and off-bounds with a series of "nursies." Dad took me and Mother to our camp in Maine every summer, to revive her nerves.

Dad topped his glass and then mine as Rhoda walked in. Sweat ran on his round red cheeks. They keep the house too warm.

————

Tara insisted on sitting between Kate and me. Dad and Mother at either end. My sisters opposite. The hundred-pound chandelier lit up the white cloth like an operating table. A massive silver fork impaled a dribbling roast. Resting his hands on his silverware Dad said, "We thank thee oh Lord for these thy gifts. . . ."

My gift was the brimming whiskey I'd smuggled into an upstairs bathroom, in case of not enough wine. But when the wine appeared I shook my head no. This drunk was starting to feel like the original kind, like high school. I didn't want to be sick.

"Russell's cutting down," Kate explained.

"Good good. Guess you all have to stay extra sharp now that Ginn's at the helm."

"Captain Queeg," I said.

"You don't stop by my office to shoot the breeze, much." Dad hacked at the roast beef. "Why's that?"

"If you ask me," Kate said, "Russell is totally overworked. They load everything on him."

From across the table Rhoda gave a clear snicker, as if she knew what I didn't—why my wife was talking for me, shielding me like an invalid. Since Rhoda broke up with her roommate and moved back to live with Dad and Mother she hardly says a word, but her expressions and noises like these are enough.

"People in glass houses," Rache quoted. She is our radical intellectual, a philosophy teacher and girls' hockey coach at a rich kids' college—like Rhoda she dresses mainly in black but the symbolic message is protest, I assume, not mourning. Rache speaks plenty, but what she means is anyone's guess. Now I guessed she meant: You, Rhoda, are a pitiable regressive parasite while (even though Dad provides all the bennies) Russell at least holds a job. I, Rache, am the only one here with any concept of real *work*.

Mother said, "Tara dear, is something wrong?"

Tara slumped. Like a little crab her hand ran to mine.

"Tara eats vegetarian," Kate explained. "For ethical reasons. Not chemical."

To my daughter I whispered, "Stick by your guns."

"Tara the totem," said Rache. Rache, the sybil.

Forgetting, Dad poured wine into my glass. "Well kids—so what's new down at the old Turner place?"

"The addition's finally getting started." Kate sat up straighter, as if cued. "Our contractor's only waiting for a thaw."

I laughed. Then I swallowed some wine. "Correction: Kate *thinks* we're putting on an addition."

Rhoda laughed too, her burpy giggle. She has tiny square teeth like mother-of-pearl chips. Her glance bounced around the table, left no one out, stopped at Kate.

I said, "Speaking of delusions, my wife is also convinced—"

Mother patted my wrist. "I've seen the plans, Russell. They're adorable. What about you, Tara? A whole new kitchen and family room—aren't you thrilled?"

Beside me Tara mumbled, "All I want is a pony. That's all I want."

"Mumble mumble?" Dad leaned forward, smiling.

"Tara *thinks* she wants a pony," I said, shooting a look at Kate, but it landed nowhere.

"Please excuse me. All of you." Kate stood up. Her napkin parachuted to the chair as she whirled out of the room, leaving it strangely empty.

"Tara thinks. Don't underestimate her!" said Rache. "Cogit ergo sum. Meaning, if you ask me, desire is the mother of invention. Or of action?"

"You tell 'em, Rache." I finished off my wine. "They let you teach that real-life stuff? About desire?" Mother lifted her glass too, as if in an impromptu toast. I saw the Beaujolais slop wildly inside, a miniature hurricane, until Mother's left hand wrapped itself around the shaking right. I watched with a chill, growing sense of shock. Remorse. So Mother knew too: that our supergirl Rache is in truth an outcast, an alien. What Dad, in crude innocence, calls a dyke.

In our family, we don't tell secrets.

"Dum de dum de dum," said Rhoda. Her fork playfully chased two peas round her plate. Normally, since whatever happened with the roommate, she hardly eats. My parents' expressions softened, and I was cheering for her too.

"Dum de dum, Rhodie," I said.

"Into each life," said Rache.

———

Bent over the trickling tap in my parents' green-and-lavender-striped bathroom, I gulped whiskey, rinsed my mouth with water, drank, and rinsed. Whiskey tastes wretched on red wine.

Each time I straightened, a startled stranger—spiked hair, dripping chin—popped up in the mirror. On the shelf below stood Mother's creams, Dad's silver razor and wood-handled shaving brush. When I pressed this brush to my cheek I became small, with Dad lathering spicy thick soap on me and beginning my "shave." And then the sting burned through. I cried out. His smile vanished. He dropped to his knees and gripped me so close I couldn't stop soap and blood from smearing on his shirt, and his grip, his *apologies:* You're not hurt, Russ, say you're not *hurt*—were what frightened me.

I heard twin sets of footsteps approaching. Mother's soothing voice. I checked the lock and torpedoed my empty glass into the laundry basket just as sharp-heeled Mother and shuffling Rhoda passed by.

Down the hall, a door closed.

I reminded myself I hadn't locked myself in this bathroom merely to drink.

A car fired and roared out. Adios Rache, I whispered. Good getaway. Then, mixed in the engine sound of my sister's car, I thought I heard the echo of another.

———

"Dad?"

He stood at the kitchen sink, jacketless. His back tensed: a little jump. "*You*. What'd you come back for?"

"Hah. Thought I'd gone?"

"Well, sure I did. We . . ."

"So do I take it my dear wife left without me? With Tara?"

"Well, it's late, I don't know Russ, she maybe assumed—"

"Don't *worry*."

I sat down at the breakfast table with a sense of not having rested in a long time. The bars of Mother's Hitchcock chair braced my spine. "I have to tell you something, Dad." Suddenly all my lies were in my throat, choking me.

Lifting a sudsy platter he tilted his head to attention. "Your mother's gone on up." He shrugged. "And Rachel had to dash, teaching an early class tomorrow, you know how she always was the early bird, but I sure hope she's careful out on those roads. . . ."

I thought: *crap.* Your daughter's driving like a bat out of hell to get away from us—back to some *woman's* warm bed—who does things to her you're too simple to imagine, who I have to guess makes her *happy.* . . . And look at me. *Look.* Look what you did! You set me up. . . . Made me think I was so goddamn special—no matter *what,* you heaped on the toys and bikes and cars and the house—you fixed my salary, my disaster-relief bonuses—Christ it's obscene, a forty-year-old on *allowance.* . . .

But that wasn't what I meant to say.

With a humorous flourish Dad yanked the sink plug. He wiped his fingers on his shirt. "Whatever's out of kilter between you and Katie," he said, "believe me, it'll blow over. A marriage is . . . a marriage is like a team of driving horses. Remember in Maine how we used to go watch the driving? Team driving's a rough sport! Maybe the pair *looks* equal but in fact there's never an equal pair, there's always your wheel horse—he dominates, he's the leader, his job is to sense what's coming, set the direction. *Wheel* horses, Russ. Understand what I mean?" Dad moved closer; he reached to open a cabinet over my head.

"Whatever's up, I'm glad you came back. I sort of missed our talks." He set a decanter of sticky amber liquid and two shot glasses between us. "Have a booster, boyo. Hey. It's just us now, sans the ladies."

"Thanks." I thought suddenly: God, you're not old, what made you retire, how could you be so selfish? Then I pictured the payout he must have received—a scrolled pseudo-antique check, like the ones I had countersigned for years for minors, divorcées, senile beneficiaries. Where was that money? Waiting for what, for whose need? In my mind I heard: Dad, I need a loan. Please. A bridge, not for long . . . A cool wave of nausea rolled up from my gut, over my head. Dad pushed my glass closer. "Thanks," I repeated, "exactly what I need. You go ahead." My teenager's sarcasm rang through the kitchen, while Dad poured himself an inch and sipped. His smile glistened.

"Well, wouldn't you say Rhodie's taking a turn for the better?"

"Better . . . ?" I stared.

"You know, Russ, boy—I can tell *you*—there's times I think we may be in for a long haul, with Rhodie. Then nights like tonight I start believing . . . well. A man does what he can, Russ, with what he's been given. Thank God I can *be* here. For her."

I nodded. The liqueur coated my tongue like melted candy.

"Your mother," he added, "is a saint. You realize?"

"She is . . . yes."

Dad rocked back as his palm slapped the table, softly. "Che sarà sarà. Listen to me! What am I mooning about? Look at you sitting there, a young guy with both feet on the ground and a wonderful family and a whole life to look ahead to—a son who *talks* to me. . . ."

He was obviously tired. Confused. He couldn't quite fathom why I had no car, but when I said: I'll walk, air'll do good, he shook his head, so offended that I let him drive me home. For a final minute we sat side by side in his Buick, contemplating the pyramid of fresh lumber. "Happy anniversary," I remembered to say. He turned a dazed smile as I climbed out.

Only the burglar light welcomed me.

The bedroom door was shut. I edged it open. I let my clothes fall silently and lowered myself to my side of the bed, like a person favoring an injury. I lay in the dark hearing Kate's breathing, which sounded too light for honest sleep, but I convinced myself she was asleep. And had no right to be.

I envied her.

I closed my eyes, opened them, the blackness stayed. What the grave is like, I thought, if we don't completely die. What drowning must be like . . .

Like a nervous miser I calculated my insurance. Untouchable wealth. Unless. Maybe the real reason to have left Kate ignorant, to leave Kate . . .

For distraction I rehearsed the obstacles. Fake a job offer. Any offer. Erase the motive. Create an accident . . . You have a practical bent, I reminded myself. That's your talent. February, March . . . weeks to prepare. For once do one thing *right* . . .

I held my hand up like a mirror, to catch the warm moist puffs: my dragon's breath.

Kate rolled toward me, sighing. The silky inside of her arm slid down my chest, and her whole length stretched close, radiant in the dark. You're awake, I thought, you must be, oh *you*—

I let my hand fall to her back and begin to rub circles,

down to the triangle of tiny moles she calls her witch's mark.
With a little whimper she turned on her belly, and I went on
rubbing while my erection pressed against her thigh, and I
smelled her perfume, even in the blackness I smelled the colors
of her perfume. My head pounded with a kind of fierce, hot
joy. The answer, I thought, the answer, oh you, how I've
missed you—

I parted her buttocks and dampened the cleft with quick
gentle strokes. She was so relaxed. With one hard thrust at the
tight dimple of her anus I entered her. It was tricky but no
harder than entering a virgin. Suddenly she tensed and cried
out "Ah—Russell, *no*—" her back arched and I almost lost her
but I held on, one hand clasped tight over her open mouth as
she bucked and squirmed. Hush, I whispered in her ear, you
will love this, you will, hush. I sang the old song: Quiet, you'll
wake the baby. She obeyed me. When I collapsed down on her
back, embracing her, adoring her, Kate wept almost without a
sound.

———

Kate was gone. Tara was gone. For days and days, it rained.
The signs of spring took all my attention, so complicated to
keep track of: warmth, thaw, doors swelling in their frames,
light no matter when I woke up, crows screeching blue murder
through the pines, melted snow sheering off the roof, drumroll
thunder.

I left the doors open, and the windows.

Once, I went upstairs. In Tara's room rain spurted in
through dormer casements, soaking the window seat cushions
and the already water-stained floor. A doll lay facedown under
the pelting rain, and dresses and underwear lay twisted like

seaweed after an ocean storm. Her pink-and-cream tape deck dangled by its cord over the edge of the desk, revolving in a current of wind.

Once, without warning, they came back, for things Tara needed from the house. In my half-dream I sensed them tip-toeing past my nest of blankets. Before leaving they paused over the slumbering monster, to look.

———

When the rain stopped I went to work inside the stone walls, in the southeast corner of the old meadow. The sun blazed down through bare branches, melting pockets of frost and drying my mud-caked shirt as I dug. I had heard the stranger approaching, feet shuffling leaves, snapping twigs, for so long that I ceased paying attention. Squirrels, louder, bounced and chittered in the oaks overhead.

"Oh my God—!"

I looked up. I smiled at a red, tasseled hat, a turquoise parka, baggy pants, mirror sunglasses. Heavy binoculars clasped to the breast. "Hi," I answered.

She stared. "Russell? Oh. You're not Russell."

I laid down my spade and cupped my chin—the lively sprouting beard—in my hand. "Who else?" I shrugged. "Who else?"

She took a step closer. "Well, you know *me*, at least."

"I do?"

"Birgit."

"Ah yes."

"Birgit *Svensen*."

"Sure. I know." I indicated her binoculars. "Out bird-watching?"

She pulled off a glove. It was complicated to shake hands, over the wall. She nodded at the first load of lumber I had brought down, roped on the wheelbarrow. Enough to start with. "What are you doing?" she asked.

"Building. Putting up a barn."

"A barn . . ."

"Small barn. For Tara. She's desperate for a pony."

"Oh. Well, *great!* We thought you—someone said there might be—some trouble? A problem?"

I took up the spade and went on digging the foundation, shovelful by shovelful, knowing she would leave soon. "No problem. Ponies aren't hard to find."

She laughed a little. "Isn't Tara a lucky girl! Ever worry that you might spoil her?"

I looked up, gripped by an overwhelming urge to explain, but all I saw was my own silver reflection, and no words came.

SWITCH

FOR A.D.

$\mathcal{S}$cotty Goodchild—racehorse trainer, licensed in four states, never ruled off track, nineteen years married—is beginning to see himself as a novice in life, a clueless liability to himself and anyone who gets too close. (Not innocent, though. Right now Scotty feels about as innocent as a backstretch hustler.) Confronting his own lack of experience is like staring at the sun: there's only a stark void, surrounded by luminous suggestion.

Scotty's mind can drift; he's cruising down the Mass Pike

between Worcester and the 495 interchange, bouncing gently at the wheel of his Ford half-ton, protected from sharp jolts by a woven lumbar pad. The geezerish but comfortable back pad and also the Celts cup holder stick'umed to the dashboard are gifts from his wife, Lil. Lil has a knack for detecting needs a person never knew he had.

Scotty is driving through the last hump of summer. New Jersey, for the past week, was holding its sullen green breath; here, although the steamy air is saturated with insects that splatter his windshield, the trees are already tinged, as if splashed with nail polish, and he knows that up north, at home, the swamp maples will be in full blaze against an ocean-blown turquoise sky.

The sky now overhead is spiderweb white. It's mid-morning, and Scotty's heading east, straight into the sun.

In the predawn dark their fingers met under the pillow where he'd buried his alarm. He clutched off the clock's peeping, then her hand funneled into his; she lay across him light and feverish-warm the way her skin becomes during sleep. Clock-tick. No wishes. No names for the outside. Nothing real except these seconds. Nothing more he'd ever fear to lose.

"Don't wake up," he said.

"I didn't sleep." She whispered too. "Oh, it's wrong, this is just wrong. You shouldn't have to go——" Her open lips crushed against his arm. Their ribs fell and expanded together. He held her, amazed by the pliancy of her bones.

Down on his left—everyone's a half-story below, except the diesels—a yellow swept-back Pontiac pulls past. It's been keeping pace since Hartford, bracketed like Scotty between sixty-eight and seventy-three, signaling and overtaking with the proper mix of conviction and caution. Scotty feels a kinship with the driver. He—or she—shares with him a certain aesthetic of order, and civility, and purpose, and also genuinely knows how to handle a car. Mass plates, like his. No bumper-sticker philosophies. Four lengths ahead the yellow Pontiac swerves back into the center lane, while Scotty sucks bitter coffee from the plastic cup (spout-lidded like the training cups his daughters were weaned with), and now the Pontiac slows behind a shimmying Jeep so it's Scotty's turn to hopscotch. This time, passing the Pontiac, he hunches forward for a glance into the right-hand mirror.

The Pontiac's window is open to the furnace wind. Scotty sees a muscled arm, color of wet bark. Shades, dazzling Panama hat. A black guy—Superfly dude—cool and no expression. Scotty snaps eyes back to the road. After his first surprise the link between him and this other driver feels, if anything, stronger. Scotty never marched for civil rights, but he marched with black guys—and bunked with them—at Fort Devens, just before Saigon imploded and they were all let scatter like livestock when the feed's run out. If in recent years Scotty's had gut reactions close to what used to be called prejudice, it's only because his attitude's been twisted by specific circumstances: i.e., the shiftless sleaze that hangs around a racetrack, minorities by vocation.

Scotty's F-250 and the yellow Pontiac are floating in tandem, wheel to wheel, no asinine macho maneuvering, and Scotty, with a vision of the world revealed underneath its mirage of threat and complexity as possibly a good and simple place, shoots a smile across to the right-hand mirror. He's aware the message can't likely be received.

This is how the year with her has changed him. Before, he could recognize only one type of love: named and bounded. Now he knows a love can slip its borders, can set off other loves the way brushfire jumps around. Before, he believed that people didn't change: what could be mistaken for change was only a shedding of successive skins, till the hard undissolvable core of a person shone through. He witnessed that paring down in each of his parents, and in his brother, too. At times— as a firefly pulse, an uncanny illumination—he's glimpsed it in his wife.

But the change in him is different. Hidden deep. Last night he dreamed—*coming off the pace, riding full gallop, no bridle, gripping ropes of mane. Leaving himself like a traitor behind.*

"Tamsen," he says into the wind inside the truck.

At first, in the explosive beginning, his own emotions terrified him. Someone else was in possession. There was a morning, before dawn, when he was called to the shed row to put a colt down. The stable helper stood too close, watching. Scotty kept blinking to steady the .38, even though he had always delivered the mercy shot with deliberate speed before. *The colt's far gone, Mr. Goodchild. No point dragging it out more. Colic's past operating even if . . .* They'd stripped the colt's name away already. Yesterday he'd been Milarkey, a gangly copper-red three-year-old. No outstanding promise—only you never knew. *Colt's in coma anyhow, watch how slow he breathes. . . .* Scotty felt the choke of crying but with dry sockets, all he saw in front of him was a black chasm. The shot thundered, ricocheting in his head, then the whole barn cracked and echoed and horses neighed battering their stalls, and the recoil of sound was propelling Scotty out across the chasm, no ground under his feet.

In the beginning tears overwhelmed him even while he made love to her. He didn't know why. It could have been tears he was driving into her cleaving body.

And there were nights back at home, midnights in the kitchen when his family slept and Scotty danced—reeling, jumping the moonbeams on the floor, barefoot so as to wake no one—with her face shining in his mind like the moon in the window.

He thought that losing control had to mean he was going crazy. But now, after a year, it's different. He's still in one piece, and he's still learning.

She leaned on the rail at Monmouth Park. The sunrise struck through her hair, reddish gold, to a fresh-raked track that vanished into white mist before the first curve. His colt was trotted out, sidling and jangling the bridle. She said, "Next week I turn forty. I'm not asking you for anything. I only want you. And Scotty, I'm not going to say, I'll die if you go away. Only I won't live, either."

"Tamsen—" The name makes him bite his lip. No one else has her brown-cherry hair, the soft hollow nape of her neck. The faint veins branching through her breasts . . . She is younger than he but not as young as she looks. She hasn't always lived alone, but she's alone now. He sees her, burrowing back for the narcotic of sleep, for his trace-smell in his cooling pillow. Then pulling on her robe. The air conditioner hums in cycles and through the Sheetrock walls of her apartment laughter breaks in, blurry talk, TV music. She swallows clear tea. Her picture window looks out on other windows and the pitching emptiness of her Sunday. Six days a week she teaches at the

Kinder Kottage, a franchise day care. It's not *teaching*, she argues, it's more like disaster relief. The kids are dumped— some nights I end up taking one home—but then they're gone, no warning. You stay on your guard, you have to. To protect yourself.

Scotty stares out at the highway that is drawing Tamsen away, erasing her, and leading him north: to his house, to his daughters, to Lil. "What the hell is *wrong* with you?" he shouts. The highway rushes beneath him like a stone river, and he feels stripped naked, blanked out, along this stretch of road is the place where he changes souls. His foot sinks down on the gas. The yellow Pontiac lags behind again.

———

Nothing beats the 250 for hauling a three-horse gooseneck, but at fourteen miles to the gallon it's no commuter vehicle. Scotty pulls off into the Roy Rogers Plaza for gas and a leak and a stretch.

In him there's a hollow ache that refuses food. Suddenly he remembers long, grim dinner scenes with his oldest daughter, after her engagement to that little puke Sorrentino broke up— how she'd sit pole straight, with her eyes unfocused and glittery, and wouldn't eat the food her mother had cooked. One night Scotty bent a fork like a pretzel to keep himself from shouting. Now he has a weird visceral sense of merging into someone much younger. Someone female, even.

From the gas pump he U's to the restaurant parking lot. It abuts a crabgrass area with picnic tables, where he can walk some. While twisting off the ignition he notices, with an unexpected stab of satisfaction, the yellow Pontiac nosing in two rows ahead.

Superfly climbs out, stomping. Pins and needles—Scotty has them in his own legs. Superfly's tropical hat is bisected by a crimson band, and the sleeves of his brilliantly white T-shirt are rolled up thin, like a fashion ad. But his blue slacks are knee-worn and spotted. The stipple of unshaven beard goes more with the slacks than the rest of him.

What Scotty sees next is the driver's seat bowing forward and then a bright surprise leaps out like a party trick: all chocolate and snow, a little girl in a white ruffly dress, with butterfly bows dotting her braided head. Another kid flies out—two of them now, skipping circles until the man makes a no-nonsense gesture. Twins! The black guy—not Superfly anymore, Scotty couldn't have pegged him more wrong—goes around to the passenger's side, where he helps an elderly lady to emerge. She is heavy-breasted and broad behind, the shape a life of hard work gives to women. Scotty's own mother. This lady wears a gray bowler, little lacquer apples bobbing in its brim.

Scotty glances up into the mirror at knobby temples. Hair wisps bleached from wind and sun. Blue and bloodshot eyes stare back: for a moment not recognizing this face.

The family are filing across to Roy Rogers. The two little girls zigzag wriggling and giggling, all demure mischief. Grandmother shoos them from the rear.

———

Out of sight, down beyond the crabgrass, is a steep slope to scrubby sumac. Scotty prefers this private gully to the hustle and reek of the men's room. A breeze from the opposite slope makes his exposed skin tingle. Birds whistle with sharp imperative longing. While buttoning his jeans he shuts his eyes, and he can feel Tamsen's warm hands, touching him. She is kneeling. Now he can glance down on the schoolchild parting of her hair, he strokes her cheek, her tongue rolls and glides, and he hears himself moan. When he turns to climb back up the slope the shimmering sky and red trees are all swinging with the violent abandon of bells.

———

As Scotty regains his truck, the Pontiac driver is also approaching. Their paths merge. The stranger pulls off his shades in a sort of greeting, and Scotty feels flattered and slightly alarmed. Is there a problem? Did he cut the Pontiac off somewhere? He laughs.

"Out on the road, sometimes it's like you're connected by a giant rubber band."

The guy gives a slow stare, as if Scotty's spoken Mongolian. Then he steps back to scan Scotty's 250, as if he's been invited to buy it. "Work for some type of horse outfit?" he asks.

Scrolled red lettering on the cab door reads, "Goodchild Stables."

"More like I am it," Scotty says.

"Hah. I hear you." Tongue poked up inside the cheek.

"Well, what 'stable' stands for—" Scotty stops. Like most trainers he leases stall blocks at the various tracks. The goal from day one has been his own farm, but by the time both girls are through college and the dream is affordable, will he still be up to the work? "Not like there's a specific stable. It's more a concept," Scotty explains. "I'm a trainer. Thoroughbreds."

"Racehorses?" His inviting smile is much younger than the rest of him. The shades do a pendulum swing. "Now that sounds exciting. Might call me a trainer, too—different area, though. Different *animals*."

Scotty nods, trying to match the man up with boxing, or tennis. Basketball . . .

"Horses. Beautiful. That's a game I know I would enjoy a piece of. From the *in*side, I mean, not pushing my money across the betting window."

Scotty wonders where the rest of the family is. Eating, still? Lingering in the air-conditioning. This guy seems like himself, a finicky appetite. "Anybody can own a racehorse," he says. "It's not so complicated." But impossible with bad credit, or any kind of record. He tries to remember where he last saw a licensed black owner.

"Sure." The guy winks. "But a newcomer like me could get rolled quick and dirty, right? I don't want to pay tuition. I hear what goes down: doping, and whatchamacallit, the ringers—"

"That's so much hogwash!" A relief, to rise to the familiar challenge. "Racing's clean compared to, what, pro football? I'm not saying nothing ever gets tried but we get tested coming and going. Myself I have *never* drugged a horse, illegally. And as for ringers? Switching the entries? No way. Can't. See, every horse is tattooed, here—" he distends his upper lip, to show where the tattoo goes, "and also blood-typed. Polaroided. *Cowlicks* counted. These are individuals. Where do you think I'd end up, if I attempted a switch?"

"Hunh." The guy looks skeptical but intense. Scotty knows the look.

"If you seriously want to own a horse," Scotty offers, slapping his pocket for a pen, "I can write you down some names. . . ."

"Nah. I'd be crazy."

But the guy doesn't leave. He unwraps a toothpick and

slips it to work between his smooth plum-skin lips. There are two more things Scotty has to do before leaving the Roy Rogers Plaza, but he can't, yet, with someone around.

Tamsen was sick, too sick to make love. So he went to the super-market for her. Pushing the cart he looked down at his hands. He'd taken off his wedding ring, for her sake in this church-and-Kiwanis town, and now the ring roamed his pocket among a mess of pennies.

At home he hated shopping. The glare, and Muzak, and lost souls bending into fog rising out of the freezer sections. But here he was happy: setting a bag of coffee beans, and then a bunch of broccoli, in the near cart. For her. What was different? He had to laugh out loud, because nothing was different. Not a thing.

The man arches back against the hood of Scotty's truck, supported by the triangles of his arms. *"Women,"* he says. "What the devil's keeping them?"

"Honest to God, those little girls are both . . ." Scotty wants to say "beautiful," but he feels funny, complimenting a strange guy's kids. He doesn't remember his own daughters ever dressed with such style and precision as those two. "Are they twins?"

"They better be." The man rolls slowly around, like a sun-bather. Now his lean hips rest on the hood. "I don't guess you're a family man." His glance grazes Scotty's left hand.

And Scotty checks the guy's long fingers, splayed on his truck. No rings—no jewelry at all, which surprises Scotty a little. "Depends how you mean."

"Don't I know it!" The laugh bursts behind white teeth, out through the nose.

" 'Scuse me." Scotty reaches to roll up his truck's window. "Just remembered this one phone call I have to make—"

"Go ahead. Do that! Only, it's too hot to lock up. Be glad to watch this truck for you."

———

The air-conditioning jells his sweat. Blond wood, plastic sword plants: the place makes him see Lil; it's like she's walking beside him, she used to keep him company on the road until after the first baby. That's what saved him, Lil saved him, he was one dumb accident hell-bent on happening, before Lil. . . .

Maybe that's what it's about, he thinks. Not about the unstoppable, unreasoning lust-yearning that took hold of him down by the sumac grove. But about one person needing, and being found and healed, and later finding out he's needed, just as absolutely, by someone else . . .

"If you'd say what the trouble is." Lil walked beside him out to the truck. Two stars hung in the navy blue sky like last stubborn dancers. All he'd told his wife was that this trip might be a longer one; he didn't say for sure, didn't want her to sense any purpose in him. Her flannel nightgown flared. She held out the steaming coffee mug, saying, "It's not my imagination. We trust each other, right? I love you, Scotty. I want to help."

He lifts the receiver, sticky from previous hands, to his ear. He punches the numbers of his business charge card, hears beeps and robots, adds the chime of Tamsen's number.

"Hello?"

"Hello."

"Oh! Where *are* you?"

"On the Pike. Past Worcester." He scuffs at deflated Marlboro butts on the floor.

She's quiet. Then: "Maybe that wouldn't seem so far away if I'd ever been there."

Her voice sounds dull and remote, like the robot voices. He tells himself it's because she fell back asleep again, not because of crying. "I guess I just wanted to . . . not say goodbye. Everything okay there?" His words come out oddly used up; he has said them before, on this same phone.

"Sure. I'm okay."

Toward his age some men develop an obsessive dread of heart attacks. If he were one of them he'd be worried now. A strangling grip deep in his chest. "Look—neither of us can go on like this."

"I know."

"Look. You move up here. Somewhere close, I mean. Tamsen? I'll help you find a job, and then we'll be able—"

"*No.* I *want* to—but that would be me doing everything and you doing nothing, Scotty, and you'd end up—understand? I can't. I can't."

For a minute he hugs the receiver to his chest. Inside him the promises unfold: he'll turn the truck around *now,* come back to her. Not risk this misery of burying what they've found and nourished and kept alive till now . . . Why can't he just *do* that . . . ? When he listens again she's telling him she's sorry, and he takes what hope he can from the color returning in her voice, and he tries to explain: he didn't mean for the call to turn out this way. I'll see you soon. Time will go faster than we expect. Think of the good parts. Good-bye.

———

Outside, Scotty blinks through the glaring heat at white pin-wheels spinning over the bed of his truck. Those two little girls have climbed in. His spirits rise with the metallic patter of their shoes.

"Everything copacetic?" the black guy asks. He still has his toothpick.

"Oh, sure." Scotty registers the grandmother, sitting in the Pontiac, which must be lethally hot. He realizes they've all been waiting, just for him. "Hey, thanks for watching—"

"Where is home to you, Mr. Goodchild?"

"Haverhill. Small town north of—"

"I know. I'm taking *them* up to Lowell." The little girls are shrieking, infected with some girl-child silliness, and suddenly the guy yells, "Yo! What'd I just finish *telling* you two?" They instantly submit. Not only quiet, they drop down like balls of fluff from the back of the truck. "Get your tails over here. Double time."

"Oh, they can't hurt the truck," Scotty says stupidly.

"Come *here*." The girls line up. Their glowing cinnamon faces aren't much alike, only equally, fascinatingly lovely. Their eyes, outlined white like the eyes of apprehensive fillies, keep shifting to Scotty, as if there's something he could, should be doing.

"It's them," the man mutters, inspecting the girls' luminous outspread palms, and shoes, and skirts. "High time they learned to *mind*." Mercifully no dirt shows. Scotty no longer believes this is the father. Uncle? Mother's boyfriend? Kidnapper? Under the slapdash imitation of fatherhood he hears a strained formality. "Now. You both better get in the car. *Walk.*"

They cross between the car rows carefully, holding hands, as if the pavement's a flooded river. Still with a proud sway in their sashed backs. For a second Scotty envisions himself hollering out to them, swinging them up one under each arm, gunning away in the truck with these two children stowed safe beside him. And what does he do, once he has them?

Maybe that's what it's about, he thinks, as the girls climb into the Pontiac, and the wish drains away. Wanting to guard everyone who ever—

There's a yip from the Pontiac's horn. Its owner jumps, glaring. "*Damn* them—wait, don't *you* run off on me. Only be a second! I have to talk to you." He taps Scotty's arm as if tagging a player, then sprints fluidly toward his car.

Scotty's tiredness is catching up. He wants nothing further to do with this guy. He's accustomed to rising early, five A.M. while training, and now he and Tamsen steal the nights, too. Talking till midnight, drinking grocery-store wine. Fetching washrags for each other's tears. Erotic power of despair. Then lying with legs tangled, taste of kisses, wine, and tears in their swollen mouths. Shared faith that the sex and the talk mattered, would lead them to a revelation, clarity, an act—

There's still the other thing he has to do. Scotty crawls up into his truck, into its held, hot breath, and opens the glove compartment. Rummages under and around the gas receipts and permits and maps for his wedding ring. Again the sweaty nauseating "what if—?" What if the ring is gone. Lost for good.

The ring has soaked up heat from the day and the engine and burns like a cinder.

Agway feed depot at Suffolk, young man looking for work, young woman hands him an application—Scotty believes in this scene. It's Lil's memory, after all, which he's borrowed, copied, and colored in. *"You flirted with me,"* Lil recalls. *"I could have eloped to Canada with you, right then and there."* What he does remember is his rock-bottom desperation when he couldn't land even that lousy job. His hands freezing onto the rail as he watched the maidens load into the starting gate, *knowing* which filly would win—and in his pocket not even a two-buck ticket to prove it.

There was a half-hour break before the big sixth and no point wandering down to the saddling area too early, trainers only make the jock nervous. Instead Scotty joined the crush around one of the concession windows. Because of his height people gave way. Some who recognized him raised a questioning eyebrow, he gave his usual reply with a shrug. The excited hammering of his heart was why he couldn't imagine being stuck half-dead in any other line of work and also why he didn't need a fourth coffee. Most of the punters were ordering beer. Beside him in the crowd was a woman, so close he could see the clean part in her reddish hair. No two people share the exact same coloring. Studying animals— their markings, angles, dispositions—sharpened him to distinctions between people. This woman didn't fit in with the dedicated punters, species of cash-heavy homeless who practically slept under the betting windows, nor did she have the beleaguered cramp-jaw look of an owner. Seeing her jostled he leaned back to create space, and the woman flashed appreciation. Brown eyes. Black lashes.

"Do you come here often?" he vaguely recalled a joke about "what's a nice girl like you . . . ?"

"On my days off." She showed the dove curve of her cheek.

"Naturally lucky?"

She shook her head with a quick laugh, and moved a step away.

"So wait—who do you like for the sixth race?"

Then she turned, looking straight at Scotty for the first time. In her left eye was a sad mote, like a tear from pupil into iris, but she was smiling. "I don't have a clue," she said. "But losing doesn't worry me. It's cheap at the price. Where else can you go and be surrounded by believers?"

He jams the ring up against his knuckle, looking straight out through the windshield, defiantly. Always a queasy moment—suppose someone is watching? The ring is too tight; his hand is puffy from heat and driving. A jabbing pain. Scotty's eyes flick toward the Pontiac—and what he sees makes him shake off the ring as if it were a wasp, he wrestles the door open and hits pavement running, the impact singeing his shins.

Flags of crimson down the white, ruffled dress. She's poised with her legs apart, head bowed, so that her blood—individual gouts, red tracks on snow—can splash safely between her party shoes.

She is silent. The wailing he hears comes from inside the Pontiac, where humped shapes sway.

Scotty crouches, hands on her starched shoulders. "What happened? Where're you hurt, sweetie? Where is he—the driver—your father?"

Sweet whiff of Juicy Fruit from her bloodied mouth. "He's seeing after *her*. And he isn't my daddy. He's Robert." Mumbling, in a voice pitched low, for a girl. "Ohh. My nose won't *stop*."

Behind her, the Pontiac quivers. Its engine is running—*air-conditioned,* Scotty realizes. That's how they can hold out.

"Come on." He lifts her small slippery hand. The way to lead a hesitant horse is by constantly looking forward, moving forward, if you once look back it stops cold. Her hand squeezes, surprising him. She follows into the chill of Roy Rogers, around the counter and foil burger packs and infrared lights into the kitchen—Scotty grabbing paper napkins on the way. She scrunches these against her face, hiding, while the manager—a frizz-haired, buck-toothed woman—clucks shame over the child, the spoiled dress.

"What's your name?" Scotty whispers.

"Lateesh," the girl whispers back.

"Lateesh?—that's *pretty!*" The manager wears an impatient frown, out of habit. At every new burst of noise from the restaurant apprehension floods through Scotty's back. Surely the driver—Robert—will come hunting them any moment. One way or another there'll be a confrontation. If Robert is innocent, then Scotty is not: if only for the moment, he's stolen something precious.

Lateesh lowers the gory wad of napkins, lifting her face to be dabbed by a towel. "I feel way better."

"You bet you do. We'll wrap her up in an apron," the manager decides. "So I can soak this dress in cold water, along with some salt."

———

Entering travelers goggle. Scotty in his dusty cowboy boots, carrying the sloshing bag in which floats the salted dress. Lateesh in her festive hair bows, and the dragging, swaddling apron.

The hazy glare distorts distance. What Scotty needs is a pair of cool reflecting shades like those shining toward him.

"So, you were inside this whole time. I figured." The man called Robert scowls, flicking at Lateesh's apron. "What's this getup? What're you playing, Nefertiti of the Nile?"

"She said my dress is gonna be okay."

"Lies to comfort you. We can write that costume off." His finger hooks under Lateesh's chin until she meets his eyes. Then he grips Scotty's forearm. "Hey. Thanks. Honest to God, I had my hands full there, for a while. That woman had me scared. I was never cut out for this job."

"You always *say* that," says Lateesh.

Scotty looks past him, beyond the Pontiac, to where the lady in gray is toddling along the edge of the crabgrass, guided by the other little girl. The man nods. "That's Miss Sharon. She throws tantrums worse than any kid. Only I have to pay attention, because she's diabetic. So we never know."

"She's our lead singer." Lateesh's husky, pre-mature voice.

"*Was,* past tense, if you and your sister keep on scrapping!" Mock scowl. Lateesh takes an insurance step backward. "Seeing you bleed is what set her off to start with!"

Scotty asks, "You *sing*?"

"Not me. They do. Gospel. Miss Sharon's a Hot Dot of the week. Moved up last week from thirty-fifth to thirteenth. Here, give me that disgusting object." He takes the slow-leaking bag.

"The 'Roses of Sharon'? We're actually extremely popular," declares Lateesh. "You *have* to have heard of us."

————

Scotty again waiting, while Robert settles Miss Sharon and her double Roses in their car. Scotty has a sense of time whizzing loose like a broken flywheel. "What's a few more minutes?"

the guy said. "Could be you're the man sent to change my life." But to Scotty it seems possible they may never leave the Roy Rogers Plaza again. Always about to leave. Can *doing* someone a favor oblige you? *Has* he done the guy—Robert—a favor?

"I'm making it five thousand."

Scotty stares. The man has his shades back on, he's leaning on the truck's hood again, tapping one foot to a syncopated beat, writing in a checkbook.

"Here, Goodchild—" he rips the check free, holds it up between thumb and third finger. "Will you please take this? You're sure five will buy me a horse?"

Scotty repeats, "*Some* kind of horse."

"One that'll run, win a few?"

"Oh, it'll run. But I can't—"

"You find me my horse. Here's my phone number, on top. Soon as you're ready, call me."

"Robert. You don't know—"

"I *said,* I trust you. I am totally serious. I have my methods." He snorts, amused. "Listen. A man knows enough to take his chances, am I right?" Suddenly he grips Scotty's right hand, tight. "What type of commission?"

"Ten percent."

"Five, tops! No, I'm joking, okay? Ten is reasonable. You got to live, too. Oh man, I feel so damned—" he slaps the side of his jaw, does a half-twirl, grinning. "Hey, Scott. I'll be *waiting,* night and day! Don't you let me down!"

Scotty lets the Pontiac pull out first. Brown sickle arms sweep inside the rear window. Scotty waves back before frowning at the check, signed "Robert D. Culver" in large curly script. Phone number, but no address.

He has no idea whether the check is good. Or whether Culver is playing some malicious prank. Whose phone number this is, or what he, Scotty, will be getting into if he buys Culver a horse. Whether he will ever meet Culver again.

The ring, scooped from under the brake pedal, glints in his hand. Pure gold. Heavy metal from pounds of dirt dug out of Africa. Melted down, shaped, and traded high.

Each trip, this last moment in the Roy Rogers Plaza, Scotty double-checks to make sure no one is around close enough to see him. He can't help imagining what he, as a passerby, would think of a man who sits in an idling truck trying to force on a wedding ring. Someone who would lie, cheat, steal? Do whatever needs to be done.

Who, with a swift whistle against the pain, shoves the ring home.

THE SUMMER SALE
YEARLING

The first time you meet Nate and Dorry you might take them for losers, trash even. Nate wears old T-shirts and butt-ripped jeans, and he talks country. You'd notice his hammy, scarred hands. Dorry's hair looks like it was hacked off with a dull cleaver, and she never puts lipstick on her mouth which is wide but downturned in a sour expression that is neither her fault nor her nature. She was in a serious car crash once, and her jaw got set back wrong.

Their house wouldn't shake your opinion. A no-frills farm-house, nearly invisible from the road, more like a shack compared to the barn behind it. Streaky weathered siding they've been meaning to paint since the day they bought the place, right? Meanwhile, since that day all the acreage around their place has been divvied up into little parcels that sprouted split-levels, fake brick fronts and emerald chem-lawn. Pools and barbeques and basketball hoops. Your developers love doing pasture land: no trees to knock down.

Their driveway's got knee-deep ruts with dogs and cats snoozing in them. The porch slants so if you drop something it rolls right off, and inside's the same, floors all warped and hilly. You walk direct into the cluttered kitchen. Then the living room; squashy bucket chairs, a woodstove, stand-up ashtray . . . poor.

———————

You'd be wrong about them.

The way I met Nate and Dorry was when Mr. Columbus drove me over to check out a Summer Sale yearling. He wasn't buying my time but it was May with the grass coming up juicy and I would have given any amount of expert advice free for a chance to get out of the city. (I don't drive, since my last fall at Suffolk. I'm a jockey. I was.) We bounce so hard over those ruts that I grab the dashboard of his truck with my good hand to keep from damaging the ceiling. Mr. Columbus guns past the house and jams on the brakes in front of the barn. Despite two bristling dogs, we climb out.

The barn sliders are open. Inside I see oak-paneled stalls, brass nameplates, bug zappers, a wash stall with hot running water. An equine palace. Spit and polish.

I say something, surprised.

"Keep your trap shut, Joey," says Mr. Columbus. "Don't embarrass me. My friends here're sitting on forty acres, straight down to the river. Know what this property is *worth?*" He says, "proptee."

I'm no banker, but I risk a guess.

"Times *three,*" says Mr. Columbus.

We are looking downhill toward the far paddocks, where a short, burly guy is moving horses around, a couple at a time, with that low-headed deliberateness that keeps even thoroughbreds calm. I wonder if he doesn't hear his dogs yapping. Then he starts latching up the gates, drifting closer, still leading one animal that dances sideways, on the end of a loose shank.

"So." Mr. Columbus stands taller. Boots a hound. Fluffs out his yellow-and-pink striped tie. "Best behavior, Joey. You're about to meet a *lady.*"

I take him to mean the filly marching up, which is an eyeful. Bright bay, slick as a copper penny, with a rump like a cartwheel and a sweet little dished face. Not that they run with their heads, you'll say—but I go for refinement. Shows the blood.

Then I'm confused. The guy has wide hips, slopey shoulders, and broom-tail hair. And earrings.

"Hiya, Columbus! Been waiting long?" The dogs roll and squeal, manic with joy. "Ginger, Masker! Will you fools please hush *up?*" The person hands the lead shank to Mr. Columbus, in order to shake out and light a cigarette. The voice grinds like permanent bronchitis. The eyes are blue, and they crinkle at me, sparkling through the smoke.

"Huu, huu," soothes Mr. Columbus, snapping the shank. The filly objects to him, or maybe to his tie. "Dorry, you don't mind I brought someone along—kid used to work for me— *huu* now, baby, easy—"

"I'm Joey. Hi." I smile, partly to show that word "kid" doesn't get to me, and stick out my good hand. She takes it, with the exact right pressure. Up close, she's the same height I am.

"Nice to meet you—" Then we both jump sideways, grabbing for the filly, who's rearing up and away like a helium balloon. We each snag a piece of halter and bring her back to earth. "Shoot!" Dorry laughs. "Dippy little dame." She trots the filly out in a tight, balanced circle. "Well, Columbus? Is this the baby? Was this worth us waiting for?"

Mr. Columbus, nursing his rope burn, judges the movement. Among a few other activities he is a horse trainer. Not the only trainer whose reputation is as much a mystery to me as the miracles at Lourdes. "Yeah," says Mr. Columbus. "I like her okay. Best you've bred so far. Joey?"

I nod, hard.

Dorry squares up the filly, strokes her, whisks away a fly. "You think—Summer Sale, for this one? Saratoga?" She looks at the ground shyly.

"Hmm." The trainer strings it out, his confidence returning. "She's what, fifteen hands? Deep barrel. Big step. You've got three months to prep her, Dorry. Pack some muscle on. *Work* her."

"Saratoga? Columbus, are you sure?"

"Nothing's *sure,* Dorry. This is horses."

When she smiles, her mouth turns down even further. "I can't wait to tell him. We knew it." She's talking to herself, burbling with excitement. "When I tell Nate—he knew what we've got, right from the foaling. Oh c'mon, gorgeous, *walk on*—" Ears pricked, cool as a Triple Crown entry, the filly ankles along behind her, into the barn.

"Betcha wish you still had two arms, to ride that one," says Mr. Columbus.

" 'You can't ride every horse, you can't kiss every woman—' "

"Shh! What're you, a philosopher?"

I shrug.

Mr. Columbus hesitates, rubs his nose, heads for the truck, and then dives into the barn. I can guess why. He would like a piece of the animal. She has that *look,* that jazzed-up, running-machine, watch-me look. I hear her inside, pawing the floor and jigging, rat-tat, over the buzz of voices. Raw yearling—no manners at all, yet.

I light a smoke, which I can manage with one hand, even in the wind.

What a place to find her.

Down the hill, mares and foals and yearlings are spooking at nothing, infecting each other. Tails flagged up, flying and bucking. Thunder of little hooves. I laugh, watching—you don't get to see them frisk like that, around the Suffolk sheds.

Then I freeze, for the second it takes to realize that the attack is just noise: heavy metal rock blasting from behind a high, thick hedge. Voices crack. Bodies plop into invisible water. Puff of grill smoke.

A soda can sails over the bushes and ricochets.

"What the hell—?" Rushing out of the barn, Mr. Columbus pulls up to glare at the hedge. "Hey, turn it down! Damn punks! Okay. Not *my* cruddy neighbors. We're outta here. Joey!" I follow him to the truck. We slam both doors. He sighs.

"Problem?" I have to shout. We roll up our windows.

"Yeah. No. My *God,* she's a stubborn—" Then Dorry

steps out into the light, picks up the can, and lobs it back where it came from, and waves at us. Mr. Columbus waves back through the closed window, with a fake sugary smile that I've seen on him before.

It wasn't that she wouldn't sell. It was that her price notion was *way* out of line, he explained, on the long drive back to town. Plus she wouldn't so much as blow her nose without the say-so of Nate, who Mr. Columbus knew from experience was a tight-ass bean counter. Plus—Dorry wanted *cash*. (He coughed the word out like a chicken bone.) That was the stupidest part, he said, and why they ought to cut a deal in the first place, because Dorry and Nate had a screw loose on the subject of cash. Aborigines, finance-wise: they owned the whole farm outright, no mortgage. They paid cash to the feed supplier, for Christ sake. Talk about risk! Every single penny tied up in those horses, in the stud fee on that one yearling, really, which was why they could never afford a vacation or even to hire somebody to help with all the work around there, which Dorry did most of anyway since Nate was driving a truck all day to earn *cash*.

He felt sorry for them. Without a professional individual to bring her out, that filly would rot. Coming from a no-name scratch-dirt farm . . .

Well *I* liked her, I said.

"Meaning who? Dorry, or her horse?"

No debt. That's one thing separates Nate and Dorry from the rest. No credit, either. Rebels! I pulled my cap down and acted asleep, so Mr. Columbus wouldn't have anyone left to make fun of them to.

———

I got their number off Mr. Columbus's books, because he trained some animals for them in the past, low claimers that barely broke even. Since the smashup, I was always scrounging for work. "Networking." I waited two days to call.

"Hyello." Her raspy voice cuts into the first ring. I beat around the bush for a while, asking after the filly and so forth. Dorry catches on. I explain I'm not looking for much in wage, more like room and board in exchange for part time. (I can't work taxable anyway, or I lose my disability.) Before she has to ask I say: Don't worry about the arm. Some jobs go slower, but I get up early.

"That'd be a major change, around here," she says. "Someone else living in. I have to warn you, we smoke. I tried the gum but all it did was give me a buzz."

"I know you don't know much about me yet but—"

"Sounds tempting. Might make sense. You let me talk to Nate."

———

I never met anyone so married. As if they were married for three hundred years. You can't imagine either of them, ever, fooling with anybody else. They even look alike, with the same brown wrinkled faces. For Dorry, Nate is the King, a hired-on trucker who happens to see through the world's crap with some kind of stupendous intelligence. (There's truth to that. The man reads, and he's got even more feisty cockeyed opinions than I do.) And Nate treats this chain-smoking skew-faced wife of his like the Princess, he brings home little surprises—smoked salmon, fresh shrimps—she can't resist. (Once I was moved in, they'd yell upstairs for me to come share. We'd huddle at the rickety kitchen table, washing down the goodies with cold beer.) What Dorry doesn't know is that Nate is saving up for her heart's desire: a snazzy computer that punches out race results, breeding records, whatever. All the big farms have this. And though Nate doesn't hurry, he never stops: five-thirty A.M. he's helping with the morning chores, evenings it's back to the pitchfork, and weekends he creosotes fence and fixes whatever needs fixing. Does most of the shoeing. No wonder the house isn't painted.

I study them. If I ever get married—big *if*—it should be like that.

I can't figure their accents. Not Boston. Midwest, maybe? One morning, while we're injecting a dose of Banamine into this overdue broodmare who's behaving colicky, I ask her.

"City kids," says Dorry. "Nate and me grew up in Albany. But we've lived a lot of places. Moving wherever the money looked better not that it always was. Nate's versatile. There's not much he can't handle."

I have to laugh. Albany: some city.

Dorry eases the twitch off the mare's nose. (Most horses don't need twitching, but this mare has a human-style fear of needles.) "We're not moving again," she says. "That's over. I'd rather eat feed corn than ever pay rent again. Now we've got ground of our own under us. Something to make something out of . . . You know, Joey. Isn't that pretty much what every-body wants?" She says this dry and offhanded, but her blue eyes are wide and soft, drifting toward the filly's stall, even though it's empty—all the yearlings out to play.

In only the past week, I've shooed two real estate sharks off the premises. They're tromping the lot lines in sharp heels and clanking jewelry, spreading perfume and promising the moon. They're worse than track touts, but certain ideas have crossed my mind. "Well, I expect if you ever did decide to sell—"

"No way!" She leans down to check the mare's udder. "She's waxing up good now, hm? Won't be long now . . . Joey, I tell you: smart people don't sell land. We never had land before, neither of us. Nor in our families. And I tell you: we wouldn't have it again, if we sold. You can hardly buy farm land, anymore."

She's shrewd. She's already looked into that.

"Yeah. Things change fast," I say.

———

And then trouble starts.

The first sign appears the next morning. I'm walking down to feed breakfast and every animal is muttering or banging in its stall, each according to its own degree of desperation. Makes you feel like the most important guy in the universe. I stop in front of the barn to grind out my smoke, and that's where I see glass. All over the place: sparkling green slivers, the more I look the more I see. I pick one up: a piece of beer bottle, the imported stuff, not your normal Bud.

Inside the barn, the Attica Uprising is in full swing, so I proceed to toss out hay. Then I buzz up to the house: alarm.

Dorry comes flying down in her bathrobe and untied sneakers; Nate's still buttoning his shirt. They're ready for action. They think it's the foaling, at last.

Dorry can be great in a crisis. Not squeamish. Dead quiet and quick to act. But now, picking up the glass, she cuts her thumb and I look away from her face which is folding up as if she can't help but blubber.

Nate is bullshit. He's going to call the cops. Kill the delinquent bastards.

"What makes you sure it's kids?" I ask.

"Look." He holds out his hand. "BB guns." Two pellets roll like dice on his palm.

After an hour, we've finally cleared away enough to lead the horses out . . . but extra careful. Watching every step.

———

That night Mr. Columbus turns up, without warning, bringing a bottle of red wine.

We talk about what to do if it happens again. The cops were less than interested, says Nate. Mr. Columbus asks why we didn't hear nothing. If there was shooting, after all. Where were those dogs? (One of the dogs is slobbering over his Italian calf-skin loafer, which he yanks away.)

"Nights, we bring them in," Nate says. "That road out there? It's growing up to be a highway. Listen." We hear the windows rattle. Mr. Columbus nods.

Dorry looks guilty, or simmering mad. It's hard to read her expression. "I went down to the barn to check that mare at midnight. She wasn't ready. So I came back to sleep, the whole five hours."

"We all sleep pretty hard," I volunteer.

Mr. Columbus pops a shrimp in his mouth. We watch him chew. "Well, my personal advice is, better put the dogs back out. Wouldn't want to see anything happen, for Christ sake—your horses turning nervy—"

Dorry nods. Normally it's like a nursery around her place, the animals are that mellow.

"Wouldn't want anything to *happen* here—specially not to that nice bay filly." Then Mr. Columbus pours everyone a swallow, and starts in again about purchasing the filly, and pretty soon, being a tactful person, I leave the room.

———

I have a hard time sleeping that night, partly because I've got a wine headache, and partly because of an idea I can't shake loose. About the filly, who I call for myself Yvette, even though you're not supposed to name a Sale yearling. (That's also my favorite name for a woman: Yvette.) She's learned some education. I've got her bit-rigged and saddled, and lunging and trotting on the line with a ground-eating powerful stride. For Sale purposes she'll be more than ready. But now I keep picturing how it would be, to swing up into that saddle. Before she goes . . . I want to *ride* her.

And meanwhile Nate's lamebrain dogs are so excited to be out loose that they're yapping their heads off till dawn.

———

By the end of June every mare has foaled safely and all of us, people and horses, are dragging around in the pit of a heat wave. Dorry's letting the horses out to graze at night, when the bugs aren't so fierce.

Daybreak is still tolerable. First I set coffee on in a kitchen where the clutter is crazier than ever, because Dorry's signed herself up with some kind of mail-order business in painted plaster figurines, and they're all over the place and break if you look at them cross-eyed. Which I do. They're all five, six inches high, pouty pink-cheeked kids sitting on daisies or toad-stools, some with music boxes inside. My pin money, Dorry says, which means *cash*. But running her fingers over these Woolworth dolls for cracks or chips, she says, oh Joey, isn't this one adorable? It's a side of her I wouldn't expect.

So I weasel my coffee out from between the cherubs and take it outside to the slanty porch where the sun is cool as a lemon and the dew is sparkling on Dorry's yellow roses, and I feel great, really hopeful and strong, like a boy starting out on an adventure with a home behind him. The dogs come snaking up to remind me they're starving, and I dole out biscuits before we set off to bring in Yvette, and work her.

The filly is coming along real good. I've got her partly backed, which is to say she lets me haul myself up to lie across the saddle limp as a sack, while she worms around to sniff my pockets for treats. She hasn't flipped out yet, but you cannot ever predict yearlings. Easy does it. I'm figuring this business out, one-handed, as I go along. And in private. I tell myself, why should they mind, let's just see how far we get, step by step—but I'm lying. They could tell me to quit. She's not mine.

On the fifth of July, my routine changes.

I recall the date because of the racket from the night before. We'd tossed out extra hay to help settle the horses, but that was all we could do, except lie awake in the heat and explosions and rockets' red glare, gritting our teeth, trying to block out pictures of noise-crazed mares kicking their own foals in panic.

At first light I get up, feeling too lousy even to work Yvette.

I sense a difference, as soon as the screen door slams behind me. The silence. Only one bird whistles, asking itself a question. Cardboard firework shells and crepe paper, blown in overnight, litter the driveway. The brindle dog looks like he's sleeping under red, white, and blue streamers, but those dogs are always up and running, once I come out.

He's dead. I lift his head, which hardly bends.

I sit down next to him, right in the dust, thinking. Pretending to myself that I'm thinking. Watching brown ants march over the upturned pad of his foot. Funny, how quick the ants know.

The other dog noses my bad arm. When we hear explosions starting up again, from far back across the river, he starts quivering and whining. It's okay now, I tell him. It's over. That's nothing but the tag end of the party.

I'm dreading the moment with Dorry. But she is quiet, looking at the dog, while her mouth turns down hard and starts to quiver. Then she says something about a shovel, and turns and walks toward the barn, slowly, like a person wading through water. It's Nate who scares me. He yanks the dog over, rubs and prods with his hands, pries open the jaw. "This dog wasn't sick. Wasn't hit by a car either. This dog was poisoned." He stands up. "Horses all acting normal, I suppose? You finish the chores already?"

I just look up at him.

"Well damn it, Joey, go find out!"

I keep staring, until he breaks it off. "Okay. Okay! I don't mean anything's your fault." He slaps his neck. It's hot already and the barn flies are starting to bite. "Know what, Joey? We could use a gun."

————

He gets the gun that same evening—from Mr. Columbus, it turns out. I'm not exactly surprised, given the trainer's broad range of connections. But I've never felt much security in living under one roof with a gun.

It's not a social call. Mr. Columbus gives Nate a few pointers on loading before he hurries out. That's when we notice the white envelope tucked under the trainer's beer glass. Probably a bill for services, I say. Frowning, Nate tries to shove the gun down into his belt, which makes me swallow hard. Then he hands it to Dorry instead, and rips open the short edge of the bill.

"Shit. That *motherf*ucker."

This kind of language is new, from him.

Dorry asks, "What's the problem? What is it?"

Nate looks like he's smelled something putrid. He lets a yellow scrap flutter onto the table. "A *check*," he says, as if he inhaled bug spray. I laugh, and then I can't stop laughing, because it's the same face Mr. Columbus made when he said, "cash." I'm making a spectacle of myself, I know, but it's been a long day.

Dorry rescues the check, and reads aloud, extra cool, blowing out smoke. "Eighteen thousand dollars."

I stop laughing. Eighteen grand, after all. Certain money. No prep, no hassle, no commission, no risk, no Summer Sale— and no glory.

"I suppose," says Nate, scratching under his chin, "we could try cashing it. Long as we've got *her*. First see if it's good."
"No way," rasps Dorry. "The filly's worth more."
It's true. She has to be. The check's the proof.

————

For the next couple of weeks we take turns at night, keeping watch. Nate can't stop talking about was it merely accidents, or the kind of destructive crazies the world's full of, or has someone specific got it in for us. But nothing much happens, and it's end of July now, with Sale week the end of August. Not long to go, so we're working on Yvette in earnest, upping her grain to the limit, keeping her in days out of the bleaching sun, grooming the copper coat till our backs ache. We all feel like once she's shipped out to Saratoga, the trouble will be over. Superstition, I guess. Mr. Columbus has his streak of superstition too: he buys two yearlings, both nothing to threaten your blood pressure, from Nate and Dorry, as if the filly's magic might rub off.

Early mornings, I'm riding her. Nothing reckless. A slow, balanced canter by the river, on springy turf. She's so young, but strong, and smart—she neck reins natural as a track pony. To be riding again . . . I don't know how to describe it. I'm amazed, how it all comes back.

Dorry's real pleased about Yvette's condition. How she's muscling up, shoulder and gaskin. After a day in the stall, she's hard to hold.

But the extra work and watches are grinding me down. By lunchtime, I'm crawling. I think about taking a vacation, after the Sale, of course. But where would I go?

My shift runs from three A.M. till five-thirty. I chose that watch because I don't want anyone else around in the early morning: only me and Yvette.

Waking up is hell. I can't face coffee at three A.M. But the cool deep-of-night air helps, and I don't mind hunkering down with the dog on the porch, with a flashlight and a smoke and a copy of the racing form. Nothing else either—though Nate and I argued, I won. No way did I want that gun with me.

At first I was jumpy. There's traffic out on the road and even people on foot at that ungodly hour. I grow ears like a bat. I hear cars pulling in and out of the neighbors' driveways, late parties. Kids camping in backyard tents, hooting and whispering. I hear the housewife next door, crying like she's been up all night. But nothing happens. Not for weeks.

————

Dorry takes the second watch. Her tiredness shows only in a shadow under her eyes, like she'd rubbed there by mistake with cigarette ash. One night I wake up late, hustle into the bathroom—the light's left on but the door's wide open—and she's still in there, sitting on the edge of the tub in her jeans and shirt, reading.

"Guess I already showed you this." She smiles, reaching up the catalog, shy.

Because she wants me to, I look at the page again. It's the consignment list for Saratoga. Each animal by hip number, birth date, sire, dam . . . and owner and breeder. There's names you'd recognize off the bat such as Highcliff Farm, Mrs. Paxson, and Mrs. DuPont. And there's her name. Same bold print.

"Go," I say suddenly.

"What?"

"Go. You and Nate both go. It's only four hours. Straight out the Pike, up the Northway . . ." I'm seeing all the colors of· Saratoga—the flags and fountains and flower beds. How all racetracks used to be, they say. There's champagne and live music under a green-striped auction tent, and Dorry sparkling and laughing, dressed to kill.

"We can't." Her eyes sweep through me like she's seeing another place, too. "Come on, Joey. That's not in the cards."

"Don't be so damn mulish! What's the *matter* with you?" I won't give back her catalog, even though she makes a grab for it. "What makes you think, if you let yourself have some fun, the *world's* going to end?"

There's a sound outside like paper crumpling. The open window vibrates a little. We look at each other, questioning. "Heat lightning," Dorry says.

"Truck," I say. Then I tell her, softer, "I can handle things here. For the couple of days."

"Joey—" This time she gets hold of my hand, the other, useless hand I tend to forget about. For a second she rubs it lightly. Then she leans forward, pressing my hand against her forehead.

Looking down on the real Dorry, her faded hair and faded shirt and the strong curved shoulders, I suddenly catch a glimpse of my mother. The way she looked around when I left. Young, I can see now. Long time ago. I shiver, because they are nothing alike.

"You're missing your sleep, Dorry. I'm going down, now. Think about what I said?"

"Sure. I promise. See me thinking?" Her smile is back. Her eyes are darker than normal. She lets go of my hand gradually, taking care so it doesn't just fall.

————

So there I am, sitting out on the porch blowing smoke at the mosquitoes and watching the dawn fill in mouse gray under a low sky that's heavy odds for rain. I decide to pull the filly in from pasture and ride early, before this weather hits. Anyone watching would have laughed, to see an ex-jock stuffing his jeans into his boot tops to ride, at four in the morning, of his own free will. And don't ask me why, either, since I'd already done what I set out to do, to be first to get *on* her, for the hell of it. (We all make these personal bets with ourselves, right? There's the you in the starting gate—and also the you up in the grandstands, watching.)

Nobody's paying me. Nobody *knows*. The filly is done, she's ready, and wherever she goes on to race, under whatever name, I'll always have the satisfaction of knowing who broke Yvette. But now I'm aware that it's getting to be like a craving. That morning ride, that smooth reaching canter through the swishing grass, over the rise to the river and back. That three-beat rhythm, hauling the air down deep in your lungs where there hasn't been any for a while. Clears my mind. I find I can't work right later, without it.

I'm discussing all this with myself, talking out loud for the dog's sake, while heading down to fetch my saddle. (This saddle I keep oiled, wrapped, and bagged. It's a Pariani won off a French kid at Calder. By far the best thing I ever owned.) I'm telling myself maybe today should be the last ride, because you've got to come down off a high, *some*time. And I don't want it to be the day that eighteen-wheeler ten-horse rolls in, collecting for Saratoga. I like to keep control.

The good-for-nothing dog bellies down, whisking the cool

barn floor with his tail, while I heft the saddle up to balance on my off shoulder. Then he strolls ahead down the track between the paddocks, dumb and happy like it's the first day of creation. Maybe somewhere outside the movies there's a dog with a sixth sense, but it's not him. The sky's shifting from steel to lead. Toward the end the dog and me break into a trot because the blackflies are hitting us like kamikazes—they always do before a rain.

What I see first is the two gray fillies (belonging to Mr. Columbus, now) hugged up to the fence, jigging and nickering. The Yvette filly, nowhere in sight, is smarter. She'll race them to the grain tub, but only when it's worth her while.

I unlatch the safety chain and let myself in, whistling for her and scanning the pine growth for that flash of shiny copper. Those other two fillies are lathered up, which is bad but not uncommon, before a storm. Spooking and rearing, and the dog is plastered against my knees. He's been horse-kicked before.

"Masker, move your butt." I hang my tack on the fence and light another smoke, against the bugs. "You girls chill down, now. Take it easy." Still no copper in all that heavy green. So maybe she's lying down somewhere, which is good for them, get all that weight off those precious legs. Even so, horsemen have morbid imaginations, and that's a heart-lurching moment, when you find one lying down.

I walk into the pine scrub. The two fillies don't follow. I'm braced for her to come crashing out of the trees any second, all snorty and unbalanced, playing her catch-me game.

The dog disappears.

There's a clearing in the trees, a soft pine-needled dust bowl that the yearlings have hollowed out from rolling. They feel safe in there.

She's lying down.

I start babbling. Soothing, pleading to her. She's alive—I know that because her eye is clear and flickers wider to me. Then the flies settle back. There is a sound through the grove like a machine idling—that's the flies that cover her like a ragged black sheet. When they shift I see her wounds. All her coat is mudded and sweaty except for those fresh pink bubbles over her chest and flank and legs, kept open by the flies.

From nowhere the dog belly-scrapes toward us, whining.

As I run up the hill the rain starts slamming down, and I think that's *good,* cool her some because her breath on my hand had felt scorching hot, burning like fever.

In the barn I scrabble through boxes and along shelves looking for the needle and the Banamine, knocking everything down as I go. That Banamine is a hell of a painkiller. I know— there was a time after the fall I used it myself. I find the gauze, the yellow salve, but no needle. . . .

"Joey? You taking a fit here?" Nate's sleep-slurry growl, behind me. "What are you *doing?*"

I turn around. I don't know what I'm doing. I want to shoot the filly full of drugs to stop her hurting. To get her up— lead her away—hide her. Before anyone sees.

She's down, I say. Buckshot. She's real bad. Nate's big hands go up to cover his face. Then I expect him to swing at me, but he hits the wall instead, hard enough to shake the planking.

Then he goes out, to get the gun.

I run after. "We can save her," I say.

Nate shoves me off. "Not if she's as bad as you're saying. I'm taking it down with me."

"Listen, Nate—hey, I've seen terrible-looking situations, at

the track, much worse—she's worth a lot still—you could save
her for breeding, for—"

"Get off of me, Joey! Get *out* of here!"

In the kitchen we're still both screaming, in whispers.
Nate's rooting in what I call the Columbus drawer, where he
stores the gun. The uncashed check lies underneath. He says,
"She's not even insured. Loss-of-use is twelve percent. Who
can afford—who are they kidding?" He squeezes up the check.
The gun, greasy, slips in his right hand. He works the safety
catch back and forth. "What you can do," he says, "is stay and
watch out for Dorry."

"Don't go down there, Nate. *Please*. Let me."

——— ——

The rain's roaring so loud in the gutters that I'm not sure he
even hears. I'd been holding my mind away from Dorry. She
isn't down yet, but there is nothing like drumming morning
rain to sink a person deeper into sleep. Now I picture her,
standing on the bottom stair, barefoot, with her downward
smile and blue, blue eyes. Asking, Joey . . . where's Nate? Is
anything the matter?

I catch the screen door in my good hand as Nate dives out.
He sees me coming and pushes me back, not too hard, but I
slip on the wet, slanted porch and scrape down the steps on my
back, a dumb comedy fall. Nate doesn't notice. He is ten
strides ahead, loping through the rain like a giant black rat,
soaked through already.

I get up. I run, skidding and pumping for air. Flash pains
in my arm. Nearly nothing left. I watch Nate outdistance
me, bobbing down the hill, fading into the wash of rain between us.

I imagine me tackling Nate, who is twice my size, and how that gun might explode between us.

I imagine him slowing up to the fence, out of breath like me—and the filly ankling up to him out of the rain. Alert and shining. Refreshed by the rain.

Then I picture my saddle hanging close by on the fence. Soaked and rainblack. Plain ruined. My own dumb fault.

————

Other than that saddle, I hadn't much more than a bagful to pack. I crept back into the house, tracking mud everywhere. And then I was gone, heading for the main road, before Dorry finished singing in the shower and before any sound rose up from the paddocks, other than the rain and cracking wind.

————

There's a rhythm to the circuit: Aquaduct, Pimlico, Philly, Oaklawn, Calder, Hialeah. Once I started moving, hitching with night shippers and rolling through the back sheds and honky-tonks, nothing could stop me. I moved fast, trying to catch up with whatever nearly got away from me while I spent one whole long summer buried smack in the middle of the Suburban Dream. Or somebody's dream, anyway.

Money came easier, once I demonstrated to a few hard-up trainers that even one-handed I could stick to the backs of their rambunctious ponies for the morning breeze. Can't kick at ten bucks a ride, that's half a C-note before breakfast. I keep enough to place a little now and then—for profit, not gambling. Only when I know what's going down.

I never went back there.

They *paid* me nothing.

The first month or so I'd sometimes get the urge to call. Tempted, the way you want a drink long past when you need. Generally I was high already and it was way past midnight, when they'd be inclined either to rip the phone off the wall or ignore it. I'd be sloshing from bar to bar in Baltimore, or New Orleans, checking the tender company for one with something I could pin my imagination on, and picturing *them*—curled up in their bedroom over the kitchen. I saw moonlight in the kitchen, the way it looked when I came down for my shift. I saw the dog flopped against the screen door and the table with mugs set out for morning: mine says "Just Horsing Around," and it's got a chip right where your lip hits.

If I called and no one answered—if they were gone from there—

I didn't want to know.

By December I was in Ocala, busier than a flea in a flophouse, working the sales preps for a change of pace. Now Ocala, with its swamps and retirement camps and overall racing fever, isn't exactly where you'd expect to find Christmas, but suddenly the traffic lights blossomed silver stars and every saloon had a plastic evergreen or a pinata and played "White Christmas" till your head banged. They did a parade with drum majorettes chased by Disney floats. Santa dumped candy on the black kids who sat on curbstones, diving for Tootsie Rolls, kept in line by mounted police. Then everybody disappeared indoors, even though the sun was still shining.

I felt low. Hoofed around town for a while, looking at the fancy stuff—seventy-dollar Stetsons and crocodile belts—in the locked-up shops. Booting candy into manholes. Squinting into ground-floor windows at the blinking trees all shivery with tinsel and, even more colorful, the gigantic TVs playing the football game. Wondering what *they* were doing. I tried to smell snow, and ice. To see Nate chipping out the porch steps and scattering stove ash over ice humps all the way to the barn so she wouldn't slip and break her neck when she went down before their own dinner lugging buckets of apples for the mares, who stomped and whinnied when they heard her coming, then stood still, almost grateful, while she buckled on extra blankets against the cold.

Across an empty parking lot, at the far end of a mall, I found one drugstore open. Nobody inside, even the cashier was hiding somewhere. Fat crepe-paper bells hanging from the ceiling shook in the blast from the air conditioner. The row of grandstand racks for greeting cards was almost empty, too. I took my time and finally picked one that looked right for her: a little boy riding a rocking horse, waving a candy cane. Dorry's not particularly religious. I anchored two bucks on the soda fountain counter under the sugar shaker, and borrowed a Bic from the display and just sat there, trying to come up with what to say.

Finally all I did was sign it. "Howdy Pardner, Have a Merry Christmas—*Joey*."

Printing their full names, that street and town, made me feel better than I had all day. I put my motel address up in the corner, but crossed it out again because by the time they answered I would probably have moved on. That wasn't the only reason. Then I reconsidered, with that same irrational jolt you get a heartbeat after you place a bet. But it would look too dumb, crossed out and written in again below. I held the envelope up against the light, to see if I could make out my own address beneath the lines.

No stamp on me, of course. I looked around for one of those coin machines and then hollered for the clerk. No answer. I went back out to where the heat was rolling across the parking lot in waves. My mood was slipping. Even the bars were chained up tight and by the time I reached Silver Springs Boulevard I knew I wasn't going to send that card. The envelope felt strange and stiff. It bothered me. On the next corner I opened my fingers to let it slide down a manhole, out of sight, along with all the wasted candy and other junk.

————

I never wrote again. Nor heard. But last week, while working a grooming gig up here at Rockingham, I happen to look out of the stall and if it isn't Mr. Columbus passing by, nosing through the shed. I reflect a minute, before calling out his name. At first he doesn't know me. Then he gives me the smile, warm as paste diamonds.

"Joey boy! I'll be dipped. You old son of a bitch!" He doesn't take my hand, which is covered with hoof oil. "Looking good, Joey. You come back North for the season?" Then he wants to know, do I recommend the chances of the horse I'm rubbing down. I shrug. I don't figure I owe him much advice.

We shoot the breeze about this and that. Winners, losers, owners, breeders. "Old Nate, and Dorry," he suddenly says. "*You* remember them."

I nod.

"Those two're still hanging in there, Joey."

"So?"

"They got a promising colt, foaled early March. Exact same bloodlines as that bay filly—you remember?"

"Sure."

"But a *genuine* prospect now: this colt. Hell of a fighter. We're all hoping. We'll see. Hey, Joey—you hear what I'm saying, with this colt?"

Summer Sale . . . ? Could be. You bet.

THE TEASER

Pushing four o'clock, and twilight already sucking color from things outside. Mike's late. Cursing the cold and her own clumsiness and in particular the black gelding and chestnut filly whose heads swing to follow her, Luce hustles around the barn. She pictures what might stop Mike from coming, ever. Some days are full of accidents, like derailed trains.

Wind twangs the rafters. Whole barn vibrates. Freezing in here, windchill minus twenty outside. Luce is no wimp—she's nineteen, five foot ten, and immune to frostbite, flu, despair. But now her duck boots drag and trip, heavy as cement.

She's supposed to prep the black for shipping out. For Mike. But meantime this filly wheels in from the paddock sporting an evil kick. Shoulder sliced like a split-up orange. Blood down her elbow and pastern to her hoof. Luce sponges icy water on the casing of frozen blood. Luce's dangling brown braids and the filly's tail are both spiked with straw. The filly sags calmly on the cross ties. Luce worries she might lurch back any minute, breaking them.

"So-o, baby. There's my honey . . . Good baby, see it's only old Luce here, steady, easy, easy . . ."

Luce is alone because Ashley, the half-assed so-called manager, managed to get herself carted off to the Emergency with a sliver of wood shaving, horse bedding, in her eye. Poor Ashley. Big frigging tragedy. The sliver must have stung—big tears slicing through the makeup Ashley swears she doesn't use—but Luce has her doubts about any emergency. This wouldn't be the first time Ashley the manager has sweetly unloaded her shit on Luce.

Though now is the pits: Luce left in charge, to deal with Mike.

Stretching one hand out to distract the filly, Luce backs to a high shelf crowded with creosote cans, cobwebby bottles of liniment, various drugs. Luce forks a gob of Furazone—viscous, neon yellow ointment—with numb fingers and begins smearing it into the wound.

Horses are weird. Either they freak at a sound, a fresh breeze, or they're ripped to shreds and feeling no pain. Or they're *understanding*? Who knows.

"So baby. No more rough stuff. In your stall. See? Got your own chow, your water—"

Freed, the filly stumbles in. Luce follows, to crack ice out of the bucket and fling the shards on the aisle floor.

"That better? All cozy? Got to *protect* yourself from those bitches out there." She means the other mares in the paddock, all older, tough as nails and bonkers from the competition.

Luce thumps her palms together, flicks on the radio, and scowls at the other horse, the one waiting to be shipped. If this animal is gelded, no one would guess. He strikes, bites, defends his space, mounts mares. The kids have nicknamed him SS, Super Stud, Studface. Since only Luce, who's always strapped for time, will lead him out, he's stallbound to boot. Now she hears him whuffling and pawing, digging down to China—or to the filly he can smell but not see, beside him.

Black and rank as the devil. Up until a week ago Ashley didn't give a hoot, informing that Studface was a donation, a freebie, just some sucker's tax loss waiting to get resold. No sale now. Last week the gelding bucked off a student, one of those fortyish beginners who squeeze into spandex britches to jiggle off their love handles at a pokey circling trot. Crash landing, broke the woman's back. She's suing. Which freaks Ashley's dad, who is a lawyer for the love of God, a city person, kind of an absentee landlord to the barn . . . Until some screwup gets his attention.

So now it's heigh-ho, off we go—in Mike's rig. Luce always feels queasy, twitchy, when she thinks of Mike. Or spots his wagon. Even on the highway you can't miss it, peely red-painted open tagalong, animals all squashed in, no straw. Saint Michael, the older kids call him. Also Mike the Spike, Glue

Man, or Mighty Dog. "Angel of Mercy," Luce tries out, messing through a box of leg wraps for four that match. Oh, those golden slippers. And swing low, sweet—Then she piles all the wraps back in again, exasperated with herself, realizing there's no sense protecting a horse's legs, prepping it to meet the killer.

Her first time handing one over: figures she'd be alone. Luce jumps to blast up the radio because here comes a classic number, "Looking for Love." So, but isn't it always Luce who brags about having the gig of a lifetime, here at the barn? Place was desperate. Even Ashley said, anything you show you can handle, Luce, you *got* it. Which Luce points out to kids who graduated with her and are now busting ass in sweat pits like Caldor's and Pizza Hut, for minimum wage . . . " 'Looking for love in *all* the wro-ong places—' " she belts out the refrain, one on one with the screeching wind. Isn't that what she tried to tell her parents, when they each came creeping around, separately, to check on her? About feeling *responsible*. Responsibility you don't walk out on.

Pitch-dark, and still no sign of Mike.

" 'Searching their eyes, looking for traces, of what. Ah'm. Dre-eaming ah-of!' Hey, is that your problem?" she calls to Studface. She clomps over to his stall and stares at him through the iron grill. What is she supposed to do? Groom him, shine him up like he was shipping out to an A-rated show?

He pricks his ears, fine, small tulip-shaped ears covered with black satin. A horse says it all with his ears; the eyes just absorb. Studface shakes his mane, flickers the ears, then points them again at Luce. Question marks. He knows something's brewing, some change in his routine already under way, because why else would Luce linger in the barn with him, not feeding, not mucking, doing nothing?

"Can't wait to hit the road, can you?" Most horses would act jittery by now.

"Hunh. Okay. You go on hoping." Grabbing a brush Luce enters the stall. Studface makes room. He's good. Pretends to snap at her leg sometimes but she retaliates by walloping his nose. Mutual respect. Now she scrubs at the manure stain on his right flank, putting her back into it, him leaning into her, too. Though Luce is what her mother's friends call "a big, strong girl"—which means a *dog*—no one can hold up twelve hundred pounds. Studface, sagging a little with pleasure, controls the balance. "Who knows, maybe you used to be a show horse—I should have tried you out—" She's not the greatest rider, but she wishes. "Hunter? Jumper? I bet you can clear a fence like—" Then Luce shuts up: in his pep-rally voice the DJ's announcing the weather.

"—temperature rising! Tonight overcast with flurries changing to sleet. But that ole mercury's gonna keep on climbing till morning, folks, would you believe fifty-five degrees? I'll take it, I'll *take* it—"

Shit, thinks Luce. You take it. And you decide whether to believe you and pull off all the blankets and you push the wheelbarrow tomorrow through frigging mud, only thing worse than ice. . . . "Hey! Cut it out!" The black horse, who has snagged her jacket with long yellow teeth, pins his ears. "*Get* over."

So will Ashley use the "chance of snow" excuse to stay away all night? Or maybe longer. Wouldn't surprise Luce; tomorrow's Saturday, the barn will be swarming with boarders, horse-crazy school kids, parents lugging toddlers, geezers doling out wilted carrots from paper bags. Saturday's a cross between carnival, day care, and a mental asylum. This stall will be empty. Luce shuts her eyes. Ashley, shuffling to the taxi she'd called for herself, had been weeping rivers. Almost convincing.

––––––––

Luce was twelve, a horse-crazy barn fly, the first time she saw Mike in action.

Though other kids got shooed home, Luce had spied from her nest in the hayloft. She thought she knew the score. The yard was as peaceful as on rest day. Mike, all business, wore cheap rope halters slung over his shoulder while he let down the ramp on the side of the red wagon.

A groom jogged up with a cup of coffee: royal treatment. The manager (back in those days a souse named Billy Brody) came rolling down from the house with paperwork flapping in his hand. Adult voices drifted up to her, dry as dust. Grim words like "navicular," "cataract," "founder." She noticed how Mike talked with his hands, sloshing coffee. She saw an Agway cap, black T-shirt, jeans, boots. Tight humpback muscles. Suddenly Mike turned, dashing out the coffee in a brown arc that meant let's get on with it, and she leaned forward, startled: this Mike, a legend and a bogie, was *young*. Sky blue eyes, sideburns, handsome as a high school hero. He fixed his cap and flashed a smile upward. Luce froze.

The groom led up two mares, aged paddock buddies. Mike began to stroke the nearest one, nonchalant, until without fuss he had exchanged Brody's leather halter for his frayed string. He flung the saved halter to Brody, like a prize.

When this mare hesitated at the steep ramp, slick with fear manure, Mike's punch on her rump sent her scrambling up.

The second mare shied as Mike approached. Brody said screw the halter, get her out of here. The groom edged around, useless. When Mike jerked her rope the mare reared. Swearing, Mike held hard.

Brody laughed, saying he didn't know the old gal had it in her.

Mike hauled back the knotted rope end, whacked the mare across the neck. She galloped round him, snorting.

"Will somebody bring me a *whip?*" yelled Mike. "I'm running late!" The mare planted her hooves, quivering, dripping sweat.

"Thanks." Mike felt for the lunge whip and spun it out over the mare's rump. She bounced sideways, then forward. Brody folded his arms. At the ramp the mare's hind legs jerked. She sank to her knees.

"*Git* up." Waving Brody and the groom to flank him so she couldn't run out, Mike began to work the whip. Left, right, left. Luce saw his muscles bunching one way, then the other, under the T-shirt. White lines flared on the mare's rump as the hairs were struck sideways. Automatically, like a full-fledged groom, Luce reminded herself what liniment to bathe those cuts in, to keep the swelling down.

The mare got a foot under her and heaved, shuddering. "Heads up!" yelled Mike as the mare plunged forward to her only choice, the wagon. The three men gripped the edges of the ramp, swung it high, shot the bolts. Listened to the hoof scramble inside. From above, Luce could see the loaded mares kick each other, frantic.

"All yours," said Brody. He reached for Mike's check. "You ain't gonna tie them?"

"What for. They soon learn standing still is best."

Luce had rolled onto her back, in sweet scratchy hay, and shut her eyes.

———

Now, heading out of the barn with a ten-pound pail of feed in each hand, she squints against the wind. Past feeding time. Mike won't be fool enough to load a horse after the light's gone. She calls herself a fool for not realizing this sooner. While Luce can solve real problems she's dense about what's obvious. Like when she blasted a boarder for not cooling out his horse— guy nearly got her fired. Like not suspecting until they *announced* it that her parents were splitting up. Like not realizing what a pain it would be to live in the same house with Ashley—even though Luce bunks in the way back, she has to fight through Ashley's slobbery to get to the stove or the bathroom, duck past Ashley's boyfriends . . . Like not being sure whether anyone likes her. Or even how she *looks* to people.

Horses whicker, hoofbeats drum in from the end of the paddock. Luce's feet, crunching ice skin, know the path. Following the fence line, she shakes grain out into separate piles on the ground. Horses shove into place. Luce rests her forehead on the rail, surrounded by their whuffling, chomping of sweet corn.

That percussion from the barn is Studface, banging walls. Mad, and afraid she'll forget him. No such luck. She still has water to haul, the barn to sweep for Saturday—maybe Mike won't show tomorrow either, maybe he has weekends off. To hope that he won't come, period . . .

As she walks back, Luce surveys the sky. Not one star to
wish on, but the wind blows soft and warmer—like an animal's
breath. Still, it's hard to imagine a thaw.

———

Not till Monday morning, while she's standing at the window
swallowing hot coffee and admiring the first cherry streak of
sun, does she get a call. Luce figures ten to one this is Ashley,
checking up on her. Ashley has managed to hole up in some
guy's yuppie city apartment, on the excuse that her frigging eye
won't heal right as long as she's exposed to the "irritants" of the
barn. Also Ashley "sincerely" wants to give Luce the "growth
experience" of running the whole show for a few days. *Right.*
But over the weekend she's lost five pounds, trying to be six
places at once and thinking of ways to murder Ashley, for
good. The phone buzzes like a trapped fly. She picks it up.

"Whitegate Farm."

"Hi, Ash! I cut into your beauty sleep?"

"Ashley's not here."

"What? Oh. Well, will she be—? Uh— My name's
Mike. Hello?" Luce has been angling for her boots while
cradling the phone, now she stops, with one foot halfway in. "I
was supposed to come by for this horse, last week?" Mike
coughs. "You work there? Are you maybe in the picture about
that?"

"Yeah. I waited for you."

"Well, I apologize, got held up. Trouble with the rig. As
per usual."

"No problem."

"Good. Okay if I pick up your animal today?"

"Today?"

"Give me two hours? I'll book it, I promise. See you soon. Hey—what's *your* name?"

———

So warm out that she only needs a sweater. In the early mist birds trill, the rhododendron leaves are splayed wide open, and Luce fears that the crab apples and dogwood will be tricked into budding and then lose everything come the next ice storm. As she descends the hill toward the paddocks—sledding in mud—the horses drift in like low clouds across the melting snow. In this unreal mellow weather she left them out overnight. Even Studface. Takes the edge off, takes the bucks out. There's even a chance Studface might load on the red wagon without too much fight. She sees him, rambling between the jumps in the arena where she left him, alone. Some of the jumps are knocked down. Hell, she thinks, you should have cleared a *big* fence last night.

He lifts his head, eyeing her approach.

Despite being swamped with work she's given extra time to the gelding—hand-walking him so he can graze the withered winter grass. Luce was never a long sleeper although now, feeling so light-headed and dry-mouthed as she primes the pump in the make-believe spring morning, she guesses it's all catching up with her. But whenever she passed his stall Studface banged the door, or gave his low restless mutter. He calls up in her . . . not guilt, of course, not exactly liking, but a sense of responsibility, as a warden might feel specially close to a solitary prisoner. Knowing that, anyway, it's not for long.

Now, leaning down to snatch gulps of the surging water, she thinks what a relief it'll be, to have him gone.

———

By eleven-thirty still no Mike, and Luce is in a rage.

"Why's everyone trying to drive me *crazy?*" she yells, heaving a bucket so it bounces off the barn door. The day help stands there with his arms crossed. Wise guy. A little girl, new barn fly, playing hookey like Luce used to, slips off to hide in the tack room. "Pick it up, for God's sake. Fix it or trash it. That bucket's been cracked for days." And then this jerk hangs it in a stall, where it leaked all over.

"Ask me nicer," says the day help.

The barn fly, who is either a Jennifer or Jessica—Luce has never met another Luce—runs back in. "It's coming! The truck you said about!" Luce gave her the job of keeping watch.

"Rickety trailer? Red, sort of?"

The girl nods.

"Okay." Luce stares at the overturned bucket, her mind blank. "You . . . Jenny? Go on up the house, take messages. *Stay* there. We can't have no one by the phone, for so long. Understand?"

The girls nods and dashes off again, but that's no guarantee Luce got her name right. She shivers. Cold stores itself, in a barn.

The day help grins. "You're sure looking forward to this."

But Luce is getting it together, thinking ahead. "Let's move, okay? I've got lessons at one. Bring out that horse." The lead shank she tosses lands at his feet.

"Hell no. Not *that* sucker. I don't get no worker's comp."

She hears rattling metal as the rig pulls in. Luce grits her teeth, torn.

"Repressed," says the day help. "That's what you are. Everybody says all you horse-nut broads are basically frust—"

Luce barges past him, whamming his shoulder. She's heard this talk before, can't fathom where men get their sick ideas. "I'll deal with you," she hisses, *after.*

Studface is staring through the small barred window of his stall, aquiver at the action out there. His coat shines from her brushing, as if he belonged to someone. Luce has no clue how old he is. "Hey, Face . . . ?" She cluck-kisses to him, and hears the day help lumber out, slamming doors. The horse seems deaf. He's seeing, smelling. Smelling the stranger-animals, she thinks, already loaded in that wagon. Her heart drops. Holding his halter she enters the stall. "Hey, boy. Time to take a ride."

He edges aside and sniffs her, briefly, before turning back to the window. Stock-still. Awkwardly, Luce slides one arm around his chest, the other up over his withers, and stands there, with her face pressed into his shoulder, for forever.

———

"Horse *looks* healthy."

"He's real fit."

"But I guess beauty is like beauty does." He's left the engine on, so the snub-nosed cab shakes and pops. Studface whinnies. From inside the red trailer bursts an answer. Through the slats she makes out the shifting shapes of two horses, plus a pony.

By concentrating on Studface—halting him square, reaching up to tweak one ear to show him she's still playful, so there's nothing to act so tense about—she can avoid looking at Mike. She's aware of black clothing: black satin jacket this time, black denims, black John Deere cap squashed into the curly hair, dimming his face. He and the day help stand like allies, sleeves touching.

BELONG TO ME 161

"I've heard about this screwball," says Mike. And then:
"You're new here?" Mike is exactly her same height. He
moves so close that she inhales his mix of sweat, machine
grease, cigarettes. Now she can't help a quick check of his face,
finding it more complicated than the one in her memory, as if
someone had traced a wobbly overlay. Only his mouth is
babyish: curvy, out-thrust lips. She remembers Elvis, the
blown-up newspaper photos of the singer who's supposed to
have never died.

Mike's attention is all on the horse. His hand, rubbing his
jaw, shades pores full of beard stubble. "Well but. He don't
seem so rank." Studface snuffles the satin jacket. "You tranq
him?" Luce shakes her head. "Hey," Mike warns. "They test,
where he's going. They test right on the spot."

"Honest," says Luce.

"So what're you looking to get for him?"

"I, uh . . . Isn't that all settled?"

"No way. I never commit till I *see* 'em." Mike strolls
around, examining not the legs, as horsemen would, but the
haunches and belly. With the same expression he looks at Luce.
"For good weight, I go two hundred. Tops."

She's interested, was always curious about the money. Does
Mike guess her ignorance? "You're kidding," Luce ventures.
"That's pitiful for this big a horse." Studface is bored. He circles out on the lead, his black coat rippling rainbows like spilled
oil.

The day help spits in the mud. Mike shoots him a frown. "I
go higher," he says, "if it's one I can resell." He smiles, for
Luce. "Hey, Fox. Think you know all about me? Think
I'm only a killer's agent? First, someone's gotta do it. When's
the last time you ate a burger? Yesterday? Think about that.

But I'm my own man, Fox. Personally I don't get off on killing."

Luce is scarcely breathing, thinking hard and fast.

"Mike, old pal, how's this weather suit you?" cries the day help, tilting his face skyward like a sunworshiping idiot.

"Un*real*," Mike agrees.

"Four hundred," says Luce. Because with that kind of stake in the animal Mike will *try,* he knows buyers, can lie a blue streak for sure; horse traders do. "Here—look at the teeth. He's young. I guarantee sound."

"But gonzo," says Mike. "Or else how come I'm here?" Whistling, he starts back toward the truck. If Luce aggravates him into leaving, if Ashley finds out . . .

"Will you please *look* at this horse?" she yells. Studface prances. Stupid fool, thinks Luce: don't blow it.

"I'm looking. What's he do bad?"

"He's fresh, that's all. Needs more exercise—"

"Jumps mares," wheezes the day help. "Mares, nanny goats, broads—frigging sex maniac."

"Join the club." Mike makes this joke without smiling, while unshouldering the rope halter he's been carrying all along. "Say four, Fox? Get serious."

"Then three. He'll make a nice pleasure mount—trail—"

"My ass," says the day help. "She *calls* him Studface."

"So, he could make a teaser!"

Now Mike's laugh explodes, straight up at the sky. "Teaser, huh? Strut his stuff to the mares, get 'em all het up and weak-kneed? So some pricey stud can poke 'em? That's the job, all right. You know a lot about the breeding business, Fox?"

He's whirling the halter around his wrist. Studface shies; Luce hauls him back. "My name is Luce."

"Three. Deal. On delivery. Means you load, and you come with and *unload*—"

"Unload?"

"Why not, he's so quiet? You say."

The day help grins. "Sure, Luce. Take a ride. Don't worry about things here."

"Hey, Fox. I want you *with* me."

———

She hates him calling her "Fox," like he's ragging her, though that's not the tone, there *is* no tone, it's more as if he can't hold on to her name, the way she can't be bothered to remember if the little girl is a Jennifer or Jessica. Leaving, she told the girl to cancel lessons for the afternoon. "Here's the list. And don't you even *dream* of riding while I'm gone," she threatened.

The girl nodded, huge-eyed. Luce was sweaty, mud-splotched, still breathing hard. Studface had loaded, but only after she'd wrapped a chain under his lip. Mike had stepped up behind with the whip. Inside she'd skidded in filth, dodging jittery animals. She managed to head tie her horse, and a scrawny bay gelding. The mare that snaked out to bite her, and the old pony, she had to leave loose.

Now she's jolting up and down on the frayed turquoise bench of his truck, trying to crank open the window for air. She hasn't looked at Mike since she climbed in. His paper coffee cup rolls on the dash, his fingers pinching a cigarette twiddle the radio dial, his denimed knee flops over toward her side of the bench.

"You want music?"

Luce nods. They hit pavement, rev to forty on the straight, with Linda wailing "I've Been Cheated" and B.J. craving that "Two-Tone Chevrolet" and then comes her all-time favorite, "Looking for Love." Mike's free hand settles beside her, tapping the beat.

"Great song, Fox. I love this song."

"It's okay."

"Not exactly a motor mouth, are you? You're my *customer,* Fox. New business relationship. I like to do things spontaneous. So tell me you didn't want a day off! Keep me company. I get sick of driving alone. Half the stuff they play nowadays is crap."

"I know."

"I get sick of being alone, period." She senses his stare. "What about you? Got a friend? Serious I mean?"

Luce grimaces.

"Long story, huh? I was married up until a year ago. *Married.* You get in the habit. Not the habit *you're* thinking, Fox!" He laughs, but quieter than before, feeling along the dashboard for his smokes. "I mean, company. Her days off, my wife rode with me. We did some long hauls. Overnights."

Luce is picturing those honeymoon rides with condemned, sick horses in the back, and thinking, I can bet what happened to *that* marriage. But she flinches whenever she hears of a divorce. Like passing a car crash. Those blue lights reeling. She wonders where the hell he learned to drive.

"Say something," orders Mike.

"What was her name."

"*Is.* Is her name. She's still around, for God's sake."

Luce manages to inch down the window so she can rest her

elbow on the ledge, turn her face to the warm sweet rush, though why it should smell sweet she doesn't know, without snow the fields are back to the rust and cream and brown of November. Gray islands of pine. She imagines time rolling backward. Almost forgets how she got here, because ever since they set out she's been glued to the radio, listening to Mike, anything to block out the thuds and scrambling that reverberate through the truck. She imagines being that wife, throned in Mike's cab, wondering when the trip will end, and how. Maybe the uncertainty excited her.

"Where are we going?"

"Her name was Cheryl. What's yours."

"I told you. Luce."

"Luce. Loose Luce, is that it?" She can't believe his hand is sliding up her forearm, pushing back the cuff of her sweater, squeezing her muscle as if taking measure. She draws away. "Cheryl didn't look anything like you," Mike says. "She was the delicate type. Blond, blond, blond. At least I could have sworn, till we got married. Normally I'm swift at spotting fakes." Suddenly his voice changes to a tinselly falsetto. " 'No doing it with the light on, Mike, not until we're married.' Jeez. She had me wrapped around her little finger. You ever been in a state like that?"

Luce wonders: Why are you telling me this?

"Hey. How come you never look at me when I'm talking?"

Luce meets his blue eyes flecked with black. He widens the tangled lashes.

"That's better. I was getting a complex you might not like me." His smile isn't nervous at all, it's winning, a smile for after smoothly switching halters. His hand glides up over her thigh, where her jeans are faded most, and into the crevice between her legs. Lies there, burning. The burn spreads over that leg and up into her belly.

The radio's doing "Love Is a Rose."

"I came along because of the horse." Her throat is dry, as if she'd swallowed timothy chaff.

"Um-hm."

"To see where you decide to take him."

"Oh, *that's* why."

"Where?"

"Haven't given it much thought, yet." His fingers are pushing the beat into her flesh. Luce feels faint. Swimmy.

"Not to . . . the usual place. Mike, you basically promised. The gelding's worth more. You agreed."

"*I* promised? Who are you trying to box in here?" His fingers stab in a way that's almost friendly. "Hey, Fox. Don't jump the gun. You seen a dime from any three hundred bucks yet?"

Luce sits very still, feeling her body cool, and her mind clear.

———

"On delivery. On *delivery*." His hand gives a pat, then leaves her, in order to swing the rig into a rutted track between corn stubble and trees. Luce grabs the dashboard as they brake. Ahead are rolling fields and copses. No fence, no farm. Behind them the road is lost.

"Gotta take five." Mike is already down from the cab, his head level with her waist. He pokes it in to add, "Back in a jiff. *Relax*."

He's left the keys. The song now playing is new. She

watches Mike fade into the line of trees, then pushes her door open barely enough, and slides through. Her knees buckle as if she'd lain flat for a week. Twigs snap as Mike cuts into the woods, but Luce doesn't look his way, hurries instead around the wagon, to the ramp. She knows the mechanism, but the bolts are high and rusty. When she whispers a swear Studface whinnies, abrupt and piercing. The wagon shakes with stomping horses. . . . She prays all the animals are still on their feet. Then everything falls quiet, except for the whine of the radio.

"What the *hell*," says Mike.

Luce whirls. There's rust on her hands.

"This truck's my property." He's still stuffing his shirt into his pants; his cap's missing and the long black curls fall forward like a little boy's.

"I just meant to . . . Maybe there's water around, some-where."

" 'Maybe there's water somewhere.' What's the point? Jeez, I *left* you the keys, you coulda stayed in the truck, you had the radio—"

Luce blushes. He's right. She had the keys, but he was too close by—she couldn't have done more than rock the rig back over those ruts before he got to her and she had pictured that scene already, with him hanging on the cab, glaring in, all patience exhausted.

"Look," murmurs Luce, "I'll make you a deal."

"Oh. Another deal. I took you for *straight*, Fox. Honest to God, I was actually getting interested."

But he's conning her, she's sure. Either he never liked her or he still likes her now. Standing in the sun, next to the slat-striped moving shadows of horses, Luce feels warmed and powerful and desperate. "I *am* straight," she says. With crossed arms she grabs the hem of her sweater, pulls it high, struggles in woolly blindness, then steps to a dry patch of grass, folds the sweater, lays it down.

"So?"

"Want to see me? You do, don't you. Right here, in daylight?"

She's facing the sun now, so his expression is invisible. "You're kidding," says Mike. He laughs a little. "Hey, you're funny."

Luce whips back her braids, one-two. "I'm wearing this shirt. Jeans, bra, pants. And boots. Boots won't count. For each thing I take off—you let out one horse."

"Wow." He slams the ramp, spins a turn. "That's some game. That's risking *money*." There's still laughter in his voice.

"Only what those other three cost you, right? *I* haven't seen a dime." She hears a song and saunters over to the cab, long strides, to up the volume. It's Lacey J. now, pleading, "Don't Fall in Love with Me."

"That's the deal." Luce springs to her clump of grass. Safety zone.

"You crack me up, Fox."

"You go first," Luce hopes.

"No way."

She shrugs. He is a narrow blur leaning against the ramp. Luce begins to unbutton her shirt. It's green plaid, from the Army-Navy, stained. She pictures the bra she put on that morning, big as a bandage, but clean. " '*Don't* fall in love with me, 'cause *that* would be a big mistake. . . .' " She hums, stripping the plaid cloth down one shoulder, then the other.

"Jeez," says Mike. "I'll be dipped in shit. . . ." His voice holds a husky edge, no longer laughter.

"Stay over there," says Luce. "It's your turn."

No rush. He makes her wait. Endless. She pictures herself as a statue, stone, larger than life. Only the sunlit side of her is warm, she's divided into heat and ice.

" 'Every heart I wi-in, is one more heart I break. . . .' " Through the song Luce hears a clang of metal and the ramp easing down. He could get kicked, she thinks. Now, framed in the opening above Mike's head, stands the pony, a shaggy oldster pinto that pitches forward, tripping against the edge of the ramp that Mike is lifting again, already. Lurches up, dazed, ambles toward the corn husks, starts to forage. Untrimmed hooves so long they curl like a Chinaman's nails. Shit, thinks Luce, you're an old pet. You've forgotten how to run.

"Okay . . . good." She unhooks her bra, lets it fall, feels the weight of her breasts. Gravity.

Mike says nothing. Luce's nipples pucker in the breeze. Finally, the ramp creaks down again.

With Studface and the other gelding tied, she expects the mare to come skittering out any second. Cautiously, Mike peers inside.

"Oh jeez. Just what I *don't* need. She's down—"

"So go *in*. Your turn. Untie one."

Scuffling, and then the ribby bay emerges, sniffs the air, shies at the sight of Luce, and canters down stiff legged, to join the pony.

Mike stands in the mouth of the rig, clasping the posts on either side, leaning into space, squinting down at her.

"Seems *your* critter don't care if he's let off or not." From up in his rig Mike sounds calmer.

"You got your back to him. Watch out."

Mike nods to the pony and the bay, now grazing near Luce's sweater. "Those two." He finger combs his curls back, smiling. "What'll you bet as soon as ole Mike whistles, they trot in?"

"We'll see."

"Okay. Let's *see.*"

Her boots are stubborn. She tugs at the laces. Through her socks the grass prickles, frosty but wet beneath. She unzips, lets the jeans slide down. She leaves them around her knees, for warmth.

"Step out," Mike sounds hoarse. "Give me the whole show, big Fox."

A new song is playing—only the bass beats in her ears as she stands statue still, legs braced.

"Turn," he murmurs. Luce twists through the eye of the sun.

Mike is silent. But she's sure, as she pivots again, that he'll keep the deal. He's not mocking. No meanness now in Mike's silence. Luce feels pure, *strong,* with the sun sweeping across her shoulders and neck and breasts. She hears her mother saying, "Straighten *up,* honey! Let's accentuate your assets!" She remembers her mother's temper snapping in the fusty changing room of a department store when young Luce refused to undress, to squeeze herself into a spangled nylon bathing suit.

She turns slowly. Windmill. Her arms are white sails.

What would Ashley, wimpy man-crazed Ashley, think of her now?

"You having fun yet?" cries Mike. She stops. From the trees a cardinal pipes, long and clear. "Shake it, Fox . . . Whooee! You are something else. Dance, baby! Hey—might be your guy's turn next."

Finally Luce sees him vanish into the red wagon. Lets out her breath.

"I can't budge this frigging mare," he yells from inside, furious.

The whole wagon sways. Hoof clatter. Snorted fear.

"Face?" she calls. "Face, you okay in there? Ready? Come on, get set . . . Hey boy." The black horse crouches at the head of the ramp, licked with sweat. "Easy up there. Watch your step—"

His head snaps one way, then the other. His eye is rolling. Whacked out.

"*Easy.*"

He takes aim at the farthest point of the field, then charges. Luce gasps in the wind of his passing. Hairs brush her bare skin. Clots of mud fly up, splattering her, and then the pony and the bay break and gallop off like they were suddenly reminded of something, till all three are specks in the thin distant mist.

"Damn it! No way I could hold him."

Luce jumps. Mike's voice is urgent, close to her ear. "Lemme look if you're hurt."

"Get *away.*"

He moves, muttering. "Put your stuff back on. That mare in there won't even—"

Luce hooks a finger into her underpants. "We made a deal, right? I'm not finished with my part."

She's shivering, after all. She'll try, for the mare. Maybe

together they can raise her up to walk. She's righteous, joyful. She yanks the pants low down one hip before Mike can grab her wrist.

"Luce—quit it! Don't you know when to quit?"

"Let *go*. It's a *deal,* understand?" At the end of the field puffs of dust rise. Studface is rolling in last year's dry corn, ecstatic, hooves flailing skyward.

"You're a mess." Still holding her, he untangles a wisp of hair from between her lips. Then snatches up her shirt. "Here. Jeez. What did you want to *do* that for? You realize, those horses will starve?"

Luce shakes her head. No.

"Hell. They'll get caught." Scrape of callus, as his grip loosens.

"Maybe." She rubs off mud with her shirt.

"Or shot?" Now he strokes her arm, the way she's seen him stroke horses, soft and insistent. "You're shaking, Luce. You know you could've got hurt, bad? And four hundred bucks—what's that, nothing? You cost me! You owe me—"

Luce shades her eyes. The horses have spread out, but they're linked, a new herd. Pines are spinning long shadows, clouds massing in the west, there'll be another storm.

"Shit," says Mike. "Where'm I supposed to haul that frigging mare? The man won't take any that can't walk off. Rules . . . they all gotta be standing. . . ."

She pretends not to hear.

"Come on. Get dressed, for the love of . . . Please. Look—" he laughs. "You beat me, Fox! You didn't even have to unload, right? Look, it's late, I can drop you off wherever you say, no hard feelings. Say so long, nice meeting you—" He forces one more laugh.

"You go along." She almost adds: this isn't the first time, Mike. I saw you once before.

Mike's eyes widen. "I'm supposed to leave you out here? Like this?"

She murmurs, "Finish your run, Mike. It is your job."

"Speak up! Say what you *want!*"

Her clothes, like her hands, are cold and stiff. She pulls her shirt on. Mike has the most changeable eyes she's ever seen. Dazzling, like chips from a frozen river. When Luce looks away from him, out to the horizon of the dappled field, the horses are going, and then gone.

BARN SWALLOWS

This night—blue velvet, fireflies, and the nimbus of lamps—reminds him of the old *New Yorker* ads for Johnnie Walker. "Homecoming hour." Or something. His mother's magazines used to lie all around the house, spilling from baskets, love seats, vanity drawers. . . . From Hank's fly-shat office window the big twin-chimneyed house is invisible, blotted out by the main barn. Those magazines hang like a patch of haze in his mind.

His drink isn't scotch but gin and tonic. No ice, no lime: pure essence of g. and t. He gulps its bitterness, ignoring floating shreds of hay and dust. The dust is clean, and anyway it's everywhere: dimming the lightbulb, powdering his arms and his oily chaps and the bills mounded on the desk. "Happy as a pig in shit!" That's his sister Sally's grinned introduction, whenever she has to bring someone in.

He isn't buzzed. Won't be. It's past eight: he rises at three A.M. on show days. Since hitting his thirties, and especially since coming back home, he can't get by without sleep, steady voluptuous chunks of unconsciousness. Now that he's riding again he's looking out for his body, the way you'd care for a stranger who fell at your door. He tells himself it's not years that count. The clock's individual. The body's clock keeps its own secret time.

Across the yard there are still shadows moving, lights, the clomp-clump of hooves. His mattress is only steps away, in the small back room, but he won't quit until the last client's car has churned down the drive. The sign in the barn that reads "Lights out, boarders out by 8 PM" is already dirt-fuzzed and useless as a meter maid at Fenway Park. "You'd better jerk their chains from day one," was Sally's advice. "Whatever they pay, bro, they don't own you."

"Hey. I'll board horses for the Devil himself. I'm trying to *build* something here, okay?" was Hank's reply. He sips. The gin burns like bile, tastes good.

A moon with peaked brows goggles in at the window. Whispers wash through the screen. Hank lifts his glass in an elaborate salute, wishing he had his hat on, to tip to those spies outside. He recognizes the husky burble of Alice Bream: isn't this one of the voices that echo in his head when he's imagining what people find to say about him? "Caught me red-handed!" he calls loudly. Various women trill back their "goodnights," and then Bream adds, "Good luck tomorrow, Hank! We'll be whooping on the rail for you. *Win!*"

"Thanks!" His gratitude startles him.

Stones crunch under their riding boots. The last car leaves, threshing gravel.

He drains the glass and bends to unzip his stiff chaps and glances up to check tomorrow's equipment—all on hooks and racks, fresh soaped, shrouded with towels. Martingale, saddle, bell boots, girth . . . In his gut butterflies rise and squirm, more like caterpillars. A little gin tends to slow them down.

Outside the tiny head of a flashlight, nodding. "Sally? Yo, Sal—" But the white light's growing toward him, anyway.

"Hiya." Mindful of mosquitoes she slams the door fast behind her. His sister is flushed from work, her sleeves are rolled up and her shirt unbuttoned, laid open, showing the vee of tan on her chest.

"Thought you'd gone up to the house by now," he says.

She licks a bug bite on her forearm. "Thought you'd passed out by now." She's only kidding. *She* doesn't believe her brother has a problem.

"Soon. Listen. I can't find my damn hat anywhere."

He doesn't have to say which hat. It's felt, leather-banded, an unspeakable color between green and brown and gray, with a drooping brim. Two months constant wearing has quick-aged it. It's like one he had as a kid; from a distance it's like the one his father wears, sunup to sundown, that hat so much a signature of tall spare-boned Henry Caulwick that he might go unrecognized, any old bald geezer, without.

Sally says, "Guess what. You'll never *believe* what's come back."

"What." He's digging through the cabinet where leg wraps are stored, though he's looked there before.

"*Barn* swallows, Hank."

"Oh." He kicks the wraps back in. "Well. It is a barn."

"I found the nest. The adults were dive-bombing me. It's *neat*. There haven't been swallows here for ages. . . . Dad thought pesticide. So, maybe you don't care but *I* do."

He crosses his arms, pressing on something inside, stilling it. He pictures swooping birds, maddened by flashlight, attacking her.

"Maybe you brought them back." She moistens her finger to scour a bite on her thigh. She wears cutoffs. Her legs are firm and wiry, bowed like his for the same reason, but her knees show smilelike wrinkles. Hidden under the marks of time everyone has an individual, constant age, Hank believes. His mother hovered around nineteen. Sally, despite her toughness and a horror-story recent history that would give the locals feeding frenzy if they knew, shows all the fresh-peeled confidence of an amnesiac. His sister's soul, he'd say, is about eleven. And what about him? Maybe this is my true age, he thinks. Right now.

"Trailer's all set. Are you all set?" Dubious, she squints at the tack on the wall.

He won't mention the hat again. "Sure."

"Five hours sleep . . . ?"

"I ride better tired. Loosens me up."

She snorts. "Oh, get that! God. What you always used to say."

———

Waking, not falling asleep, is the letting go. Who am I? Where? Hank wakes hours before dawn and bucks off his mattress to slap the alarm silent while his dream scraps scatter like fish. He bumps furniture and the snoring refrigerator and opens a narrow door to a lidless toilet, cathode blue under the window's predawn. His urine splashes with pent-up force, the only sound of life. This is how it feels after the Big One drops, he thinks: or how a zombie feels called up from the grave. Thoughts he's had, waking, before.

He mixes instant coffee under the tap. Drinking this grit he smiles, because the five horses he will show today—two boarders' hunters, his father's two long shots, and Sally's big jumper—have come drumming into his mind. He pulls on britches, women's nylon knee highs, then the skintight boots, custom Dehners. He groans, swearing and hobbling with pain.

Once the boots are on he's calm. Not one butterfly. He reaches for dress shirt, jacket, tie. Black kid gloves. He reaches for his hat, remembers, and feels himself incomplete again, yearning. It will turn up, he decides. In the trailer. Or maybe Dad took it, by mistake.

"H.C. Jr." is stamped in brass on the cantle of the saddle he now lifts off the rack. "Henry Caulwick, Jr.," the announcer will say, when he rides in. (At his first show since coming home, an unrated February indoor, the voice surprised him by adding, "Welcome back, Hank." He aced every class that day.) It's his name all right but diffuse, shared, part still in his father's keeping and part buried with his parents' firstborn—a tiny angel who one day simply stopped breathing. Hank heard the story when he was little enough to believe in fairy tales. He understands how the loss must have hung too close to risk the name on the second son, his older brother, Seth. Then came Sally—a Sarah for their mother—and then he was born. He saw their reclaiming that name as a matter of obdurance, of resurgent faith.

Trailing reins he kicks at the office door, breathes the cool foggy yard. His hard hat dangles by its elastic band from his elbow. Even at four A.M. there's light. There's *always* light, his mother used to say, you have to train your animal side, though, to notice. She trained him on night rides through their woods and the neighbor estates; he had his first pony then, Mr. Snickers. He remembers trying to see color—water, his pony's dapples, bachelor buttons by the road. Once when they came in elated and sweaty his father stood waiting, wordless until Hank sidled into the kitchen. Then while Hank crammed his mouth with leftover dessert the argument exploded like a summer squall outside. "Well it's not so much *him* I'm afraid for as *you!*" his father's voice snapped like a stick. His mother's answer flowed sweetly, ending with, "Oh, go to hell." And Hank felt a shock of pride for her, and humiliation for his father, and he stood rigid with his dry mouth full of cake he couldn't swallow, unreasoningly afraid for himself. For them all.

Now, crossing the yard, the only color he makes out is the yellow backhoe, a looming steel-toothed monster. But powerless. Suspended animation . . . a Disneyland float. The backhoe quit in midjob a month ago. The job—an 80 by 120 schooling ring, graded, sanded, and drained—was a lure promised by his father in writing, before Hank came back. Hank in turn dangled the lure to prospective boarders all through spring while his father hemmed and hawed because of bad weather, extortionary bids—until one morning Hank trotted in from the field to find this backhoe churning a cyclone of dust. His mare shied; his heart soared. He watched the ring take shape: trash heap of boulders at one end, cones of sand blooming at the other. A few days later, not knowing what he was witnessing, he waved at empty trucks filing out the gate. . . . Nobody waved back. Dust settled. The noise had stopped.

"I'll mind my side of the business" was his father's only comment. "You tend to yours. Go on. Dazzle me."

There's prize money in the Open. Ten thou, six to the winner. He doesn't have the winning horse yet, so not a prayer. . . . But there's always a *prayer,* and every class today will count, every mingy ribbon, because each ride better make a goddamned *impression*—enough to switch this backhoe on again.

"Hey, sleepwalker! How about dumping the tack somewhere and *help?*" His sister's voice sails out of the fog, high and bright: anything can happen, it's a show day. When all three were kids, exempted from church to compete their ponies, he used to share that nervy confidence. Maybe still does. In his gut a butterfly circles and settles, fanning its wings.

"Never praise the day till evening," was always their father's terse good-bye.

He wakes up, obeys her, thrusts his equipment into the cab of the silvery van she's parked facing roadward. In the barn lights flare. He hears gutteral nickers and the thud of falling hay, rush of water into buckets and rattle of poured grain, as if Sally had multiplied herself into two or three, to get the work done fast.

He enters, blinking. "All taken care of," she calls. "You worry about your own." A shadow moving on.

But his mounts—the three hunters, two jumpers—are

already fed, he sees, their legs swaddled in the thick cotton shipping bandages.

"Thanks, Sal—" He clacks stiff kneed down the aisle, past too many empty stalls. One, swept and scrubbed and bolted, still bears the nameplate of Seth's last hunter: Success Story. Not that Seth rode much after starting Amherst, but there was never a question about keeping Seth's mount, and Hank, who commuted to the barn daily from his local dummy ag. school, had witnessed the animal's creeping obesity, its sad loss of tone. The preserved stall—this fucking *shrine,* he had screamed on the day he came back after nine years' trying to forget (but he had been hung over then with paranoia, torn between a conviction he was touching the swamp bottom of failure and a flip-flopping joy over the resurrected big chance)—this stall now only occasionally brushes him with nostalgia, and that is all it's meant to do. What he never remembers is Seth at the end. Their last drive. No one laid blame. In a way he no longer feels it happened: not to him.

"What can *I* do?" He's peering in at the black jumper whose oats dribble from whiskered lips. The coat so shiny it looks waxed. This is Sally's pride and joy, a prospect she hopes to campaign someday after Hank has trained it up. *Freebie* she calls him, this animal dumped on her as a parting bribe, a kind of unmarriage settlement, by the son-of-a-bitch grand prix star she dragged her ass around the circuit for, season after season. Until a last shred of instinct told her the passion was turning lethal, and she had to save her hide. One of those coincidences: a week after Hank's return home Sal pulled in too, stony broke, towing in a U-Haul her trunk and saddle and the groggy black horse. He's seen the bruises that haven't healed yet, pale lavender, where her ribs meet her spine. He thinks a horse, no matter how talented, is lousy compensation: she should have sued the pervert, crucified him. An idea he hasn't abandoned, either. A possible source of cash.

Her shadow falls over the horse's flank. "Hank, come see the babies," she begs.

He would have mistaken the nest for a wasp hive. Would have blasted it with long-range Raid. It's a drooping wedge of gray wattle, glued to a joint in the rafters.

"You're taller. Can you *see* them?"

He tries. As he stretches up on cramped toes an adult bird arrows past, wheels, followed by another. Now he sees over the lip of the nest: gargoyle heads, all gaping yellow beak and bulgy eyes, screeching and straining to poke farthest over the rim. An adult hovers, pumps a bug down the foremost throat.

"Aggressive little suckers."

"Cute, huh? How many?"

"Three . . . nope. Four."

"Good. Now you've seen them. Let's go."

This show lies south, almost to Rhode Island. Thirty miles live load makes an hour, in the van. That's nothing. To hit an A-rated show they drive easy four, five hours each way, because A-shows are where the truly testing courses are and also the best judges, veterans like Chapot and Morris who make their calls regardless of past favors, past record, rumor. Judges Hank needs to be seen by.

Sally drives skillfully, her muscles sliding under dry brown skin as she shifts gears, all her attention focused backward on the heavy but vulnerable cargo, lightly chained, rocking on braced hooves, behind them.

———

The young girl has frizzy hair, slanted hyacinth blue eyes. "Put it away," she says to Hank's dollar. "Before eight the coffee's free." The yellow canopy tints her table, the trampled grass, like sheltering sun.

Though the coffee scalds his lip he smiles back, because her blue eyes won't leave him. He feels the awkward warmth movie stars must enjoy. In the girl's eyes he's a pin-up hero: a male rider, a jumper-rider by the white of his clean but indelibly scrape-stained britches.

"But look," Seth argued once, "It's not a *guy's* sport." They were high school age, then. "Twenty-five to one you get your ass whipped by a debutante. The odds are grotesque." Seth's excuse for dropping out of showing, though he still fox-hunted, where you can throw yourself over fences like a sack of bran. Seth never had much form, anyway. Later Hank began to wonder—involuntarily, not wanting an answer—whether Seth was maybe gay, already or becoming. He had no exact evidence, only a needling premonition that had to do with Seth's glibness, his soft, slipping, successful way of dealing with life, the *differentness* between them.

Their mother said, "It's the *boys* who make it to the top. Meantime, what's wrong with being rooster in the henhouse? You meet these wonderful girls—"

Spandex britches reveal every swell and pucker. Lady riders—keyed up, weathered, joking, handsome—are crowding in with brisk excuses, lunging for coffee. The girl behind the counter wears a T-shirt cropped to reveal a tiny colorful decal just above her navel. He can't decipher the winking

design. "Care for anything else?" Beneath powdered peach
blusher, she blushes.

"Another coffee?"

"For your groom?" Her irrepressible smile. He hasn't
touched a woman since he came home, not for six months
before that, doesn't masturbate either, too tired. Before, he was
too busy poisoning himself—too sick. But as a kid Hank
Caulwick had streams of girls. And then there was Lynn, eons
since he's given a thought to Lynn, though friends called them
"as good as married," which was still a far cry, thank God. His
loss of interest in Lynn, or in sex period, was simply one of
those things among many and not connected to the accident
but something that happened to him later, gradually. He leans
forward on the table with wrists pressed together. This is a hell
of a moment for the urge to return.

"Careful," the girl says, nudging his coffee forward,
tamping down the lid. "Guess you know it's hot." Her decal
resolves to a rainbow, with a star. "Turn so I can see your
number? Oh, fifty-five! That's *lucky*. I'll watch for you, okay?"

———

Sally's by the van holding his first horse, a walleyed pinto, property
of Alice Bream. He trades his sister slopping coffee for the reins.

"Beautiful. He's a plowhorse, not a hunter . . ." No matter
how much the world's rich, fat Alices pay him to ride out their
fantasies, he hates this part of the work: campaigning a loser.

"You can make anything look good. You've still got the
eye, Hank. It's gotten *better*. I'm jealous—blindfolded, I swear
you'd find the spot." The elusive invisible magic spot, she
means, the ideal takeoff point for a perfect trajectory over a

fence. There are infinite gradations in misses, from barely perceptible to full somersaulting crash, but only one spot.

"Jinx me. Thanks loads. Okay, give a leg up. Ah one, ah two—"

She boosts him into the saddle.

The five foot or so height of a horse's back changes everything. Perspective. He gazes out over the tents and three toy-like jump rings and whinnying horses being unwrapped, fresh horses bucking on longlines, to far up the road where the dust of incoming, inching vans mixes with the last low layer of fog. He smells trodden damp earth, hay, bug repellent, new manure. The P.A. system blasts earsplitting gobbledygook: Alice's pinto must be deaf.

"Bream turn up yet?"

"No. Maybe she got lost? Hope."

"Sleeping in." Hank grins. "You think she's a lush?"

Sally shrugs, rubs his boots with a rag. God, she takes care of me, he thinks. Few pro grooms could handle five horses without fouling up, flipping out. Sal won't. *Why?* I'm the one who should be taking care of you, he thinks, looking down, and the words ring distinctly, unspoken.

Casually he asks, "Any sign of Dad around?" Because it is not a long drive, and he has been searching for a tall, stooped, hatted figure, standing alone off to one side, since they arrived.

"You *want* him? Or is that a threat?" She bends double, to oil the pinto's hooves. This is a bum's job, he realizes, or a young kid's job—he envisions, briefly, the girl serving in the tent. But shouldn't this oil-smeared sister of his be someone else by now? A lady of—incredible—thirty-eight—

With the clean end of her towel she slaps his knee. "What're you laughing?"

"Me?"

"Shoot, don't be nervous. . . . Hey. If Dad decides to crop up he will; that's how he always was. If I could predict *him* I'd write the Farmer's Almanac."

But he did used to come, Hank remembers. Suddenly he would be standing there, watching from ringside but apart from the crowd, when I won.

"Know what, bro?" Sally is wiping spit off the pinto's muzzle. "You've got the same face on as when we were kids, right before you hopped off and made me hold your pony so you could barf in the bushes. Come *on*, Hank."

He gazes down at her, incredulous. That never happened.

"*Also*—" But now the P.A. crackles out the standby call for pre-greens. Sally pulls a snoot, mock-kiss, as he squeezes the pinto forward, settling his cap, aware that she will soon follow.

And her "also" follows, too. *Also,* brother, piss or get off the pot. *Tell* him: you need cash, damn it, if you're going to make this thing work, also some respect; you want that backhoe rolling again and maybe one *good* horse, not all his rank oat burners. . . . He *knows,* he just keeps you dangling, what a waste—you've got *me.* He's not the Pope so just cut that rope—

Hank looks down at his arms: wool sleeve, inch of white cuff, black gloves seemingly immobile but following the pinto motion as the ground, a hazy scroll, rolls away below. Fine, he answers. Fine, for you. Easy for you to say.

———

Alice Bream in a green dress balloons through the crowd to join her horse and rider in the winner's photograph she'll treasure like her first prom corsage, her autographed Reagan—

"Like my *divorce* decree!" she giggles, blowing a kiss into the pinto's mucusy nostrils. "You're a champion, baby. Mommy adores ya!"

Later she's the green core of a group whose eyes, only the eyes, swerve toward Hank every time he passes.

"Congratulations. But I saw you stick in those spurs. Wonder you didn't draw blood." Sally takes the heaving pinto and hands him a jittery chestnut mare. "Next victim?"

Overhead the sun has the whole blue field to itself. Removing his hunt cap is like lifting an upended bowl of water—sweat streams down his face. He ruffles soaked hair. He's sickish from the heat and work and not eating, but won't eat, never will before his rides are done. He needs his hat. The hat floats in his imagination, solid, within reach. He's worn it every show since the season began. It floats at eye level, elegant and battered, casting a cool circle of shade on the ground.

———

The mare chips for sixth and then jogs lame so that's that. Losing can be an advantage, the bracing edge. . . . Hank's next horse is a bay called Fanfare. Before Hank can tighten the girth Fanfare rears with no warning and coming down nearly clips Sally's skull as she dives to save the fallen saddle. Hank shivers. Grooms run these risks. . . . The horse is entered working hunter, a serious three-foot-six division, but it's a *cheap* critter, cheap blood. His father's horse. Buy for a song, let Hank school 'em up, sell top dollar. That to his father is the venture, the whole crapshoot deal.

Two rounds over fences equals sixteen spots to be found riding a brain-damaged animal which, as they enter the ring, is already bent on yanking Hank's arms from their sockets. Hank touches his cap toward the judge, but it's the plainclothes dope testers, he suspects, who will be taking notes on this action.

A freak first place. Next round earns fifth, but Hank scratches out of the third class, because this is the kind of horse that gets crazier and crazier until it literally drops dead. Back at the van the testers are waiting: two neat short-haired women, ultrapolite. Sally strips Hank's saddle off the bay while the testers draw blood. "Still no Dad?" Hank asks.

"Right." She blows hard at a flopping hank of hair. "Like I've got nothing better to do, than *look.*"

She's crashing, he thinks. That's all her trouble is. He discovered crashing long before he smoked his first joint: how the glory promise of early morning evaporates in the heat, the stress, failed equipment, unforeseen bad luck. Not always, though. For Hank, this show's hardly begun.

"I'm worried about that gimpy mare," Sally murmurs.

He spreads his hands in sympathy. The P.A. announces a lost child and that the Open will start at two. An hour to go. Faraway in ring three the jump crew is already setting candy-cane rails, man-high. In Hank's arms and legs there's a tingling, as if the butterflies are colonizing there. The weakness is numbing, almost pleasant.

"I wish you'd *eat,*" Sally moans.

"Now's the break. I'll get you something." He passes the testers, one of whom calms the bay while her partner kneels with an outstretched arm holding a glass beaker under the animal's flaccid sheath. Fun job. "You might be here all day." Hank frowns sympathy. "That critter doesn't have the brains to pee."

———

Under the tent swarm dogs, wasps and flies, riders whose white shirts cling transparent to their bare skin. Recognizing no one Hank moves freely in this fellowship of strangers. Like a lover the frizzy-haired girl rushes toward him, tripping on an orange electrical cord; she wants his order. Her eyes are teary and brilliant from the smoke of the grill. Does your rainbow mean anything? he asks her. She lifts her brief shirt another inch, as if the mark were a complete surprise to her. You're doing so good, she says, I keep hearing your number. How come I never saw you around the circuit before?

I was away, he says.

What circuit? Florida? I'm going to look out for you. Everywhere. Henry Caulwick, Jr.? *Neat.* I'm going to look for you in the magazines.

————

"Hurry up and wait" is what riders murmur to each other in the warm-up area or idling on dozing horses by the in gate while the sun advances in its sole and perfect arc. But Hank, walking the course now, counting strides between towering flagged obstacles, feels it the other way around, feels time compressed, dragging like lead weight on his boots. He goose-steps like the others, but there's no fellowship here in the ring: every rider, lips twitching with the count, is alone. Their eyes hug the ground marking dips, stones, grass slicks and also because it can be paralyzing, to look *up* at these jumps from the ground.

A forward five strides to an easy three, roll back to the two-stride, change lead, gallop the straight, single oxer and hang a blind left—hold hard, then let'm go through the triple . . .

That's one way to read it. But now they're clearing the ring and Hank has no time, time's already cantered up fast behind him and is gathering speed, and all he can do is grab mane and go with the runaway.

Even Seth once admitted that a well-built course is like a work of art: an expression of infinite possibilities.

"Here. *Drink.*" Sally points a thermos at him and he drinks. Cool tea dribbles down his chin. Sally's toweling his first jumper, which he's just warmed up: a blue roan Caulwick Senior picked up in Virginia off the timber races, cheap. It was during that buying spree that Hank's father wrote, after long silence, to invite him home.

Sally controls the horse merely by a loop of rein over her wrist. The buckle's a bracelet, glinting. "And we've got barn swallows this year," she is telling a groom beside her. "It's like nature's recovering, like stuff is real, again—"

A cold qualm ripples Hank's spine. To stand bareheaded in the glare after the effort of warm-up jumps can give you a kind of false fever. Closing his eyes he sees the nest again; fuzzy, flat, featherless heads so crowded together that it's hard to tell one from the next, inconceivable these raw peeping hatchlings will have space to grow. But they will grow. The adults are elegant creatures—gunmetal blue and crimson, fearless acrobats—like a separate species. When Hank was little it was his mother who led him up into the loft to admire the nests. "Watch for the bullybird." She could laugh in a whisper. "See how one shoves in front and takes all the food? He'll grow fastest. The parents don't even notice! See there? See?"

Time's a runaway, in full bolting flight. Sally gives him the leg up—leaping out of range of this monster-roan's stomping hooves—and Hank is working to charge the horse up even further, demanding complete attention—he's spurring, checking, spurring harder, all in a tight three-meter circle, and if the in-gate crowd is backing off with disapproving sun-bleached stares he could give a damn, as long as they know enough about horses to stay well out of his way.

He is seeing his own hands, muscles near to splitting the glove seams, and also the alternating sway of the roan's withers, and most of all the crest, the long black-maned neck that rises like a steep, tarry road in front of him, because he wants this sucker to give in, come *down*, all his work and sweat is for that moment of submission when the mouth will soften to the bit, and the spine rounds up beneath him meaning: I'll carry you, *yes*—but he has no time. Without breaking stride he glances up and around, scanning the drift of spectators for a tall, old man, rakish in a broad-brimmed hat.

The steward booms: "*Okay,* boys and girls, Bobby's on course! I've got Julia on deck, Anthony Wilde in one, number oneohtwo—where's oneohtwo?—in three, Hank is four trips away—"

Hank, then. Working the roan (shoulder in, haunches in, lighten *up,* you sucker), Hank feels the spurt of happiness of a boy chosen early for the first-string team. He used to play soccer, baseball, lacrosse; soccer was his best game. *My* theory, Seth said, is sports are like languages: the more you get under your belt, the easier the next one is. Seth won the Latin prize all four years; he read philosophy in German and dirty paperback novels in

French. Together they used to hike high behind the cornfield with a pack of Winstons filched from their mother's purse: Seth would puff and cough while talking about pacifism and Sartre and Martin Buber, and "I and Thou." And Hank inhaled with smooth precision until his head began to float, dizzy from watching the corn tassels dance, and from the "I and Thou."

"Clear round for Bob! Eighty point thirty-three seconds is your time to beat! Way to go, *Bob!*" Clear but crude, in Hank's opinion. Scary deep to the oxer jump, and if the horse hadn't torqued his hind end that whole bank of rails should have tumbled. *Nice horse* . . . His own animal's back suddenly begins to fill and hump beneath him, the crest rounds down to accept the bit and just as swiftly Hank gives slack, scratches the quivering withers and murmurs, " 'At-a-boy. You pay attention to this next one."

Nothing's changed. This show's a tradition, fifty years or so. Same tents pegged down in the hollow, same officials as when he was here last—when?—ten years ago. He was taking a flyer with his father's big hunter on this jumper course, and they predictably demolished it. Caulwick Senior who watched from ringside spoke not one word, after. Of course his mother wasn't there. . . . Horrible now to remember his *relief* realizing she couldn't be. Was safely gone. (So natural, they said, like it should be, she simply slipped away, under the oxygen tent.) She died in the nick of time: to spare him finding his defeat in her eyes, magnified, shared. . . .

The second time he felt grateful for her being gone, he had more right. After the accident, with Seth.

Who *had* been here that day, ten years ago, he suddenly recalls. Helping out, as Sally's supporting him now . . . If I ever got pissed off about Seth, he thinks, it was only *about* him, the whole situation. We never said but we knew we were lucky to be good brothers. Even in fights we stayed careful, I never hurt him. . . .

With rueful tenderness their mother used to describe her children to other adults, as if the children couldn't grasp her language, couldn't hear. To Hank this was her private code: revealing her heart by pretending he wasn't there. . . . "Hank's our youngest, the proverbial surprise. Isn't there always one you can't quite bring yourself to let go of, let grow too big for good-night hugs, and kisses . . . ? He's a cutup, though, Hank is. Act now, think later, not that our oldest lacks self-confidence, he's the determined one Seth is, still waters run deep, how I sometimes express it to myself is if I told Seth to leap off a cliff he would, trusting, whereas Hank would jump, too, but Hank, I swear, would *fly*. . . ."

"You're on deck." Sally shoves his stirruped leg aside to brush sweat from the roan's ribs.

"Yah. Okay." But he's lost. Like a fountain the butterflies rise into his chest, stealing breath. For the hundredth time this day Sally buffs his boots.

Whereas our Sally . . . But Hank can't remember their mother ever finishing the thought about Sally, only her deepening dimples and a swift glance skyward, as if the whole story were there.

"They've been pretty cautious, most." Sally means the rounds, till now. "You might—" She sucks in audibly as the rider on course charges into the triple only to meet with refusal, pitching forward to his horse's ears while the animal rocks on planted legs, nearly going down. The rider recovers and circles, lashing ferociously, for a second try.

"Jerk. That didn't have to happen," Hank says.

"You got a plan? There's room." Room to move up she means, and maybe place, within the best time.

"Feel it out. How it rides. This guy's green, Sal, he's for practice. Your horse is the one who'll get the ride." At this moment Hank doesn't usually talk, is in a trance, but now he's talking to himself.

With the panicked rider hauling rein the second refusal is inevitable. Last try.

"Thank you," soothes the steward. "Oneohtwo, thank you, you're excused—"

Hank's roan dances crab-wise, evading the grip. Hank swings his flat palm back and whacks one, hard. Sally smiles. "Bye. Have a good trip."

"Fifty-five. On course."

Posting into the ring he sees not the jumps (puzzle cutouts, towering illusions, he has already studied them to death) but the path between: his approach, the turns, the precise strides leading to the magical, shimmering spots and all this is like a picture book he once had, where when you laid a colored film over one image, a secret fantastic one emerged from the page.

The buzzer sounds. He opens his circle. Lifts into a canter.

In the ring time expands, boundless. His vision becomes unnaturally clear. Curving past the in gate he sees his sister's sun-reddened eyes and also beside her the young girl whose hands push up her cheeks and frizzy ginger hair in a gesture of . . . anxiety? Delight? He can smile, there's only ice inside him now, even his own smile can't distract him.

Even at this compressed slow-motion canter to the first obstacle you need a sense of acceleration, of the horse firmly in front of you, the fence must be a distant desire you strain toward. It must never be the fence that comes for you.

The roan pats earth and rises up with Hank crouched securely in the arc, beginning to jab spur for the forward five. Clear. Clear. Left rein, collect, roll back.

The next day he went back to look at the nest alone, even though climbing the loft alone was forbidden and the babies were like gray tiny mice but opened their beaks piercing and shrill sensing his nearness, but he counted only three—one was missing, and anxious he dared look down at loose scattered hay and there was a scrap like gray tissue paper with beak and long pink legs, and later his mother explained why, sometimes the others will try to push a weak one out; it happens that's nature sometimes—

Out of the turn forward to the first hurdle of the two-stride. The roan squats and lifts off, balanced like he's got twin jets, behind. *Long* stride—they do the two in one, shaving tenths off seconds, and gallop free of the combination. Clear. Shit, thinks Hank, *shit*—we could win this class. Nearly half the course is negotiated now and the thought hits like a sweet megasnort, or the explosive high of love.

Collect. Hip shift. Look up now, pressure left, right— *change,* you sucker!

In the momentary suspension of the lead change he sees a dark stick figure, propped on a cane, hatted, outlined against a field of green. *Good. Forward.*

Some horses won't hint at half of what they've got until the chips are down: on course.

So watch this, Dad. You'll love it. You're nobody's fool, you've got an eye for horses, after all.

Horses, Seth said, it's so ironic, how they're some kind of aesthetic symbol. Until you get up close, right? What bugs me is there's no *purpose,* no *end,* it's simply this inarticulate class ritual that just goes on and on—look at the getup you have to wear, like a pantomime. And what it all costs, what you could do with that money—it's so egocentric! But the whole thing's sacred. The equipment hasn't changed in a hundred years—

We were talking about the farm, Hank interrupted. Hank was driving; Seth slumped beside him. The more excited Seth grew, talking, the limper his body—except for his waving hands. Hank didn't know where they were going; Seth directed, it was Seth's graduation weekend, all milling, beaming parents and long tepid luncheons at long catered tables. More than once Hank had seen Seth droop, pensive, he guessed because their mother wasn't there. Let's get the hell out awhile, Hank had offered. He wanted a beer. Escape, Seth had agreed.

Okay. *About* the farm—

Seth. What he said last night is, *you'll* own it—

Don't get hung up! Sally's not, is she? We'll work it out, share share alike, remember? I'll need you, bro, I always will, and I mean, we can make a *dif,* we've got to try, we can grow food, build something, it's a lot of *land*—The road uncoiled ahead, a smooth river reflecting the sky. Hemmed by flashing green and silver windwhipped leaves. Hank gave gas in the curves, for traction, thinking how all these mountain roads looked alike.

Gallop, damn it—the oxer ahead is an orange and white mountain, banked rails like steps to the sky. Stay tall, don't commit your body ... Heel jammed so deep the stirrup irons cut through leather. There's the spot, now open this stride and from here on never look at this jump it's certain, eyes up, look over—

The stop is like a blow from a giant hammer. His bones sing. His crotch smashed against the pommel and the spectators' gasps of thrilled empathy echo his own gasping. The oxer, within arm's reach, is a blur. He's blind, winded.

The roan throws a rear and buck that send Hank twisting upward and then like some freaky blessing back square in the saddle. Whack the bejasus out of this roan hide—! All right. Regroup. Gallop forward, pull up, canter on. Circle. Time's blown. Steady, now. Take the long approach.

And while they drove Hank kept his mouth shut, too parched imagining the bliss of beer, while Seth who would graduate next morning summa cum said look, I'll be closer to home I'll be at Harvard I can help you Christ listen to me yuk I'm not so smart no smarter than you only it's time to put kid stuff behind you remember that's from the Bible, remember? Oh, remember in Sunday school Miss Dempsey how you told her you were Buddhist not Christian because no way you'd go sit on a cloud and miss out—you wanted to come back a *horse?*

And Seth was cracking up, and Hank smiled with his lips pressed shut feeling the generous warmth of the pale arm flapping beside him, understanding once and for all how anyone—their father—would have to love Seth deeply, his brother. And he drove on shifting skillfully, longing for beer, his head reeling from all the mirage of colors and thinking what a fuckup he was—

And now the orange oxer is approaching fast again and he sees
the strides ahead clear as chalk marks on the grass but doesn't
quite believe, but *has* to—reaches back for a whipcrack and the
roan shudders, staggers. It's ugly but they're *up,* they're clear,
they're over.

Blind left. Tricks in this course. Next time I'll *know* . . .
Hold now, hold, collect his power for the triple, steady . . . *Go.*

Going into the next curve he braked first then accelerated
racestyle maybe showing off a little but correct, knowing
how to make speed work for him right on the edge ready
to shoot free on the straight while Seth's arm wobbling
with laughter and exhilaration gripped the dashboard—

This is *fun,* Hank shouted feeding gas sure of the turn
though it kept unrolling bigger than expected then something slipped, the car flew out twirling free like an amuse-
ment park ride through the clawing and snapping
branches—

And Hank saw the tree among all the other trees:
slender and pretty rushing toward them fast and he hauled
the wheel in midair trying to make that tree his own but
the car was falling left, left and the tree when it came
cracked into his brother's side, into Seth, instead.

"Okay. Don't move. You're okay. Someone go back for the
stretcher? What's your name? Can you feel this? Here? Move
your fingers? Good. Your toes? Hold it. Just lie there—don't
move." The voice blurs, changes. "What happened?"

"His back." Sally's voice is very close. The sun is directly
over him, engulfing, but she's somewhere close by. "He like
flew up and over and slammed into the rails. Hit with his back."

"Okay . . ." A siren whines, lost, faraway. "Let's just keep him real still, miss."

Somewhere someone else—a little girl?—is blubbing.

In his head he's been speaking for a while but no sound comes.

"What?" asks Sally.

"Ah . . ." A drink. Something. Shit. He lifts one arm and touches his lips, which are scaly and dry.

Salty rain of unleashed tears.

"Don't *move.* Jesus Christ. Jesus Christ. I watched you, Hank. You—*why?*" She sounds angry, the way some women turn angry when they're scared.

"Give me . . . minute. Cath my . . ." He tries to smile, to find a word. "Still can ride. Your horse. Next."

No answer. There is, instead, an eclipse of the sun. Slowly a curved shadow descends over his eyes. Pitch-dark. He reaches with the arm he can move, inviting pain, and touches the felt grain of the hat, its complicated shape. His fingers explore dents he doesn't remember, but it could be his hat.

Else his father's.

He'll find out, but right now this darkness is all he needs.

IF WISHES
WERE HORSES,
MY LOVE

"Lord, send me a clean break," declared Twomey. Foremost in his mind was his lady friend, ex but unable to accept the past tense. His thoughts dived a level lower to his viciously paranoid ex-wife. Touched on his own greed-ridden parents, next, and then sank deep down to Connaught: Ireland herself. He rolled a toothpick no-hands from the expressionless left to smiling right side of his lips. "Once the party's over, isn't a clean break the one hope a man has left?"

No one listened. The clash of conversations and cutlery
and the string trio tormenting the al frescos outside on the ter-
race wiped out Twomey's words; moreover, he was alone at
his table. Through the checkered glare of the Royal Saratogan's
salon he made out a thirsty crowd milling behind a silk rope
barrier: jockeys, beauties from the City, grooms, bond pushers,
drug traders, young punters and old, all tossed together in this
small northern New York State town for the annual Meet. No
one tried to claim the three empty chairs beside him. He imagined (or caught) certain individuals recognizing him and swiftly
averting their faces. "You'd all rather starve than have my sort
of luck rub off, wouldn't you?" Either that, or they were afraid
he would try to sell them a horse.

He was expecting Mr. Crocker, since well past an hour.
No mistaking the man: six foot three topped by a plaid
sportsman's cap, cadaverous shoulders pole-stiff as though he
lugged the original Cross under his powder blue jacket. Not
likely—for one thing, Mr. Crocker claimed to be a lawyer.
Astonishing confession, if true. Lying bloodsucking spawn of
Judas that they all were. Not so long ago Twomey could have
used a lawyer of Mr. Crocker's probable stripe; now it was too
late. Twomey, bored and preoccupied and nervous, dipped
into his third vodka and tonic. The ideal summer drink.

Mr. Crocker, though late, would not disappoint him.
Crocker wanted something, had been mousing around
Twomey's stalls ever since the Meet began, dogging Twomey's
steps on race days from shed row to track and back again like
an old pally schoolmate. And in fact (it often worked this way
with women, too, the playacting sparking a genuine affection),
having spent time with Mr. Crocker over the summer,
Twomey had a soft spot for the man whom Marianne (merely

for example) dismissed in her small-town snobbery as "the uncouth Albanian." Albanian? Because the man lived in Albany? Uncouth? There were his chain-smoked Marlboros, and the gold rings and necklace. And Mr. Crocker drove the Wheels: a 1978 maroon Cadillac with smoke-gray leather interior dominated by dangling fuzzy dice so huge they obscured the road. Over the rutted mud tracks of the shed rows, the low-slung Wheels billowed and bounced like an Emperor-size purple and chrome waterbed. Grooms stopped and stared, nodding respect. Afternoons, propped at the bar among trainers who unlike himself were Saratoga veterans, and who implied past experience with Mr. Crocker and his ilk, Twomey found himself spending a word for the Albanian: "There's many sorts of class. There's working-class class, a rare thing around here. The man is absolutely proud of where he comes from." At that, some stranger had sneezed into his beer.

Munching Spanish nuts by the palmful, squinting out over the rim of his greasy glass into the glare of a hanging light that made his blue eyes water and identified him loud as a headline— TWOMEY!—while the crowd entering and circulating remained dim as the dead. Mr. Crocker he would not miss. But Marianne? She might be wearing a man's three-piece, or a velvet gown, or buckskin with fringe. Her gold hair pumped up like pastry was unmistakable—but she might fancy a hat. "Ah, you ladies all dress to disguise your, your—" he paused, and a dimpled child with five silver studs marching up one ear returned his wink in passing. Marianne would not dare come in. A week ago yes, to sob or scream at him as her mood might dictate. But no longer. If she now chanced to look in at the Royal, hoping for friends, and spied him before he spied her, she would turn tail and run. Turn her extravagant broad tail, and tumble back down the ostentatious dirty outside carpeted stairs onto Broadway's sidewalk, and dash away through gangs of tourists, stumbling under the ripe-to-bursting harvest moon.

Tiresome. After a certain age some women go hard, but most go sticky-soft. Twomey couldn't deny a sense of commiseration with her husband, that same abusive s.o.b. whose guts a knight-errant Twomey had dreamed of skewering for the first intoxicating months of tupping Marianne. . . .

No regrets. Bottoms up to the good and devil take the dregs. "Timing is all, love," he reminded the absent one, with a rueful smile and shake of his head: Twomey's own coppery locks on the wane and overdue for a trim, but the color inborn, not poured out of a reeking bottle. Heaven's witness, he'd waited nearly three seasons for the lady to make up her mind, scrape together her courage. Twomey the adviser. Soul's comforter. Afternoon stud. She had her kid to consider of course and went on about that, but truth is, money's a difficult thing to wave off. Who would have expected now, after all his faith had been worn away, that she would send Mr. Tightcheeks packing? For that matter, where was the proof that she had?

Twomey snapped his fingers. A waitress dumped more Spanish peanuts into his bowl, but that wasn't it, it was that the child with earrings reminded him of Nat, Natalie, the new exercise rider, Natty B. he called her to her charming, friendly, oh-fuck-you-old-goat incomprehension. "*Natty* were here, love, she'd send these fat-bombs away from me!" The waitress grinned deafly, indicating her ear. Twomey patted his prominent tum. His American tum, an ever-growing, demanding entity that had latched onto him like a succubus, or like Chang the Siamese twin—presumably during the passage through Kennedy customs. American-style, Twomey could pitch the blame: career stress. The volatile climate. Or his "home," a nineteen-buck-a-night motel far up the Northway. Penury. The lost, say it, *lost* fight to keep his parenthood—his Moi. Moira, his heart's own darling. When a father *loses* his daughter—

Twomey fist-guzzled peanuts. He blamed himself.

Natty often stole the coffee rolls and burgers right out of his hand, as if that were part of her job. Only yesterday morning the exercise girl had lisped to Mr. Crocker, "Guess what. Twomey's on a seafood diet now. . . . The minute he *sees* food—bam, he eats it!" Crocker had looked baffled, politely suspicious. Natty lisped: "Theafood," she'd said.

"Irish." A heavy hand sunk into his shoulder. "Been holding the fort long?"

"No hardship. Enjoying the local attractions." For a moment Twomey wasted his smile on a massive silver-scrolled belt buckle. Then Mr. Crocker's midsection swung away to reveal a woman in the awkward half-crouch of seating herself. Fancy turnout, he noted: velvet pumps, sheen of panty hose pressing the blood from her plump knees, a silk dress with a floppy low cut and something to show. He thought, *What in the name of Hell? What the goddamned—*

"Bon soir, 'sieur Toe-*may*." She gave him a mournful, sideways look.

"That's right, forgot you two know each other! I bumped into Marianne at the Wop's," Mr. Crocker said, scraping his own chair up closer. "Split a great lasagna. You ate long since, I take it?"

Twomey nodded. His tum hurt. Ample on the outside, empty as a cathedral on the inside. Suddenly he remembered, though Mr. Crocker evidently did not, the introduction: Twomey's own doing. Back in July, was it? Early morning, steam-kettle fog over the track. Stopwatch. Ears and eyes straining, and then Forever You, classic bay and full seventeen hands at only three years of age, hurtling in a mud cyclone out of a cloud to flow ghost-dim into the next. Mr. Crocker had grunted, hardly hiding his lust and excitement as he wiped prescription Ray-Bans. "Three and change," Twomey might have noted aloud, writing the time. A moment later Marianne hustled up to them from her Eddie Bauer Bronco, pink under fresh makeup, licking her lips, exclaiming how she couldn't wait to hop on her horse Forry herself, some time very soon. Crocker looked impressed. *So you ride, ma'am?* Twomey shivered, recalling her excuses to avoid so much as leading a racehorse to the paddock, and he took her hand. From that moment on he would no longer believe the lies she had told him, and told anyone, and would continue to repeat with conviction.

"Meet the proud owner," he'd said, presenting Marianne to his friend.

Wretchedly careful, they'd always been. What could Mr. Crocker have ever guessed?

———

Moi prays for Dah to come swing her up high, make the sky swirl, lift Goat-girl to sail on his shoulders again. Although she might already be too big now. And when she was little, she was afraid to look down at the shrunken ground, and to feel the big snorting steaming animals butting her toes, and Dah's voice vibrating from between her desperately hugging legs saying, *Moira, love, just say hello to the lovely lady! Give Dah's friend a peck now!* And therefore Moi, stiff as a toy, whining the way she's learned to from the spoiled American children.

"Twomey, if for one minute you think I planned—"

"But I thought that fellow was a hundred miles beneath you, love." Twomey's dread come true, to be left alone with her. Mr. Crocker, mumbling, had wandered off into the crowd on some business or other. "The Albanian?"

"What?" Blue eyes blank as spoons. "But Mr. Crocker's been a complete gentleman. He understands my—he's *very* sympathetic." If nothing else, she was a petrifying actress.

"Is he that?" And tonight her escort as well, her unwitting witness. Twomey could hardly heave her out into the street. He waved for another round, as if full glasses would exert a mesmerizing pull on the vanished lawyer.

"Twomey? No offense, but you don't look healthy. At all." Her pout of fake concern. A woman scorned keeps her little knives handy. "Have you seen your complexion in the mirror recently? It screams blood pressure, to me at least."

Marianne's lipstick tonight, the hue of a Disney cartoon sunrise, reminded him of one of her maudlin tales: about the blossoming "media" career she'd sacrificed to marriage and motherhood. He'd swallowed that whopper, deaf to her shaky grammar and occasional stunning ignorance, dazzled by her virtue, the sexy sheen of this big, high-colored, filmable woman. *God almighty,* he thought, *I worshiped the ground beneath your feet.*

"Anyway, surprise. I saved something for you," she said, reaching into her bag. "I've been carrying this around since—"

"Whatever it is, you keep it, love. Please. I don't want anything."

Her handbag snapped shut. He watched her puff up, in tiny

increments: the eyes, the rose-orange lips, the fingers (indentation where one ring had been recently removed), the soft, large pointy-nippled breasts he had suckled on starting their very first time between the sheets together. He shivered, suddenly revisited by his blind gratitude and bliss. Circe-as-sow, herself.

"Everyone in town," she hissed, pulling her chardonnay off the waitress's tray, "knows why you've been avoiding me. They *all* know you owe me money."

————

Moi's ninth birthday feels like moving to a new country. "9" is a scrawny, alert, searching number, completely different from roly-poly "8."

Moi's birthday wish list: 1) a Playmobil Victorian house, 2) any porcelain horse from Mousetrap Miniatures, the gift store in the Olde Forte Myers Malle, 3) a Greek myths book, 4) a Gameboy, 5) pastel glitter pens.

Mom gives her the awesome dollhouse with furniture for each room. Also five glitter pens. Nana gives her the Gameboy and fifteen dollars flat inside a Far Side card. Moi said no thanks to a party, because she doesn't know any kids. After three slices of chocolate cake she is slumped on the couch showing Nana how to play SuperMario. Both laughing. The air conditioner drips and chugs, trying to suck all the wetness out of the new condo. Impossible. Every street here, all the way down to the curved wall that stops beach sand from blowing over Manatee Drive, is new. Moi guesses why Nana moved them here: because it's so far from Dah: now he can't even figure out where Moi is. That's why he doesn't call anymore. They don't explain, but they don't hide the reason either: that

Dah does bad things, will try to make her do something bad. They're wrong, but Moi can't argue. To even say Dah's name is rude.

Today she's been thinking about him too much. She grabs the Gameboy from Nana and starts punching all the buttons hard at once, laughing like a nut head. It's a silly way to play. No chance to win. The card slides off her lap, to remind Moi that she has fifteen dollars, enough money for *two* ceramic horses. Moi gets up on her knees and hugs Nana's neck with one fierce arm. I love you, says Moi. You and Mom take *good* care of me. The neck skin smells like sour yogurt, but against Moi's lips, Nana's pink, scrunched-up cheek tastes like sugar dust.

———

"*Five* yearlings, you conned me into buying! Of which the three that couldn't run you sold off half-price, and then the filly *you* said was a world-beater colicked so bad we had to put her down. And I was sorry for *you!*"

"Shh, now." He wanted Mr. Crocker back more than ever. He had an idea forming: a wire-to-wire winner.

"And now Forry's all I've got left to show. Two *years* I've been paying your padded bills—" Without missing a beat she switched from their failed investments to his failings as father. "And all I did for you with Moira? The custody hearings? I technically perjured myself, trying to help you win custody! But wasn't I like a mother to Moi? While you were out drumming up business, using my connections . . . Oh, Twomey, you took the best part of me, the part no one can buy back. You must have been laughing all the way to the bank—except of course you never made it that far because you spent every minute and every dime at the ticket window and on women like that tramp you're paying to—how long have you been screwing *that* foulmouthed teenybopper? *Exercise* girl, yah. She's young enough to be your—"

"Now *stop* it. You're saying terrible, untrue things, Marianne. Things you'll regret." Twomey struggled for breath. It wasn't her insults to Natty that disturbed him. Nat was centuries tougher than this one. Not a drop of sentimental blood, which was part of the fascination . . . *Sounds like the ragged bitch is having hot flashes again,* he could hear Nat saying. And laughing until the quivering, red back of her throat showed. Twomey drained one glass, and in the relative silence picked up his next. "Are you out to destroy me, spreading this talk?"

"No."

"What then?"

"You *owe* me. I'm on my own, do you know what that means? Tell you one thing. I'm taking Forry to a new trainer. *Tomorrow.* Don't try to *stop* me."

She snuffled, childlike. Soon he would see the tide in her turning: she cupped her wineglass in both hands like a big flower, a tear fell in, he sensed her gratification at the effect. The bag yawned wide again and offered out a connected series of tissue papers like a magician's endless scarf. Marianne blew. Something fluttered free like a white leaf and sailed sharply sideways as Mr. Crocker returned.

"Oopsie!" said the lawyer, bending to grab it.

"Good catch," Twomey praised, and automatically held out his hand.

The photo was a Polaroid: square, with a lower margin to write on. In the picture, their faces flattened by sunlight, their hair blown to one side, stood two children with arms entwined. One wore a short brown tunic, the other, saggy jeans. One girl had brown curls, the other was fair. Apart from these details they were nearly indistinguishable, squinting at the photographer with gap-toothed grins. On the margin was printed: *Devon and her friend Moira, Lake George.* He could recall no excursion to Lake George. "Age five, were they?" he asked.

"Six. About to start school. Go on. You can keep it."

He covered the photo with both palms, as if it were a French postcard or an inside tip. Slid it down deep into his breast pocket. "I will. Thanks." Aching inside. That unshakable fierce ache that wrung through him, whenever the child rose to his mind.

Marianne looked completely composed again, like a film that had been rewound. Mr. Crocker was jotting a memorandum to himself on a napkin.

Extraordinary, thought Twomey. How the drink relaxed her just so, and his humorous stories tickled her, or more likely the simultaneous attention of two men. She calmed down and played her best part: the naive and charming country mother. Then, miraculously, she was yawning, and Mr. Crocker had escorted her to the Bronco, and returned with a smile twitching on his gaunt face. Surely an omen. Twomey's luck was lifting.

Now, midnight past and the night air finally cooled down, he and the Albanian strolled along Broadway. "The reason Forever You hasn't raced much," confided Twomey, "is I've been saving him. He is that kind of quality." A fresh palpable fog hushed their steps. "But—he's entered next week in the maiden allowance. Mile and change."

"So if he's running for a purse of sixty, how come you'll sell to me for thirty-five?" Crocker's voice had gone gravelly, from the fog or mistrust.

"Look. I'm not saying Forry will win this time out." Modest assessment. Sober reservation. Twomey's words falling extra soft, to compel the other man's attention. Then a laugh: "But to be truthful, I'll be buggered if he's not at least up on the board!"

Mr. Crocker hawed. "That a tip? You settle for third?" He forged on toward the parking lot in the galumphing American gait, difficult to match. The business was done, Twomey felt, as good as *done*. Thirty-five thousand American dollars, green and fresh as grass at lambing time. He wanted to stop and dance on the empty wet pavement.

"Marianne," said Mr. Crocker. "Will she sell?"

"And isn't it my task to advise the lady?"

"I heard from somewhere that you and her—you and her—"

"So tongues wag, do they? Nothing in it. Look, I tell you what! You come watch the colt gallop. Morning's not far off."

They paused on a curb for the "walk" light, though the streets stretched empty.

"If I do buy him—*if*—I don't see any reason to change management. You get on great with the nags."

"And wouldn't that be absolutely up to you, Mr. Crocker. As owner? Of course."

———

Moi can read maps. Dah showed her how when she was little. Finger Lakes. Elmont. Saratoga. And Connaught, Dublin, Newmarket, all where she's never been.

Mom and Nana can talk about Dah whenever they want. Nana said, *That golddigger never wanted you, doll. When he got you pregnant, he knew exactly what he was after. You were his Green Card, baby, I told you then. Golddigger! He abused you same as this poor little sweetheart here—*

Abuse. That dumb word. In school kids shouted it all the time. Cafeteria food fights: "No fair, you're *abusing* me!" Even Moi and Devon had to laugh. That powerful word hurled everywhere, and no one to say what it means.

Neither Mom nor Nana have time to drive her to the Malle. Moi sits cross-legged on the bus-stop bench, a street map of Fort Myers slung knee to knee. The spidery shade of a skyscraping palm is no protection. She's wearing sandals, dumb white shorts, a twisted plaid halter. Her skin wishes she had even less on. She reads the bus numbers from the map, looks up at the wrong numbers on buses that pull in, wheeze out hot tired air, and pull away. She is patient, waiting, sure of her facts.

A shadow sharper than the palm tree's blots her map. A voice possesses her ear. "Y'all lost, lil' girl? Where y'all headed? Let's see there. Might be I can be some help."

"I'm not lost. I'm fine, I don't need help." Folding up her map, Moi stands and moves away from the bench to the curb. Her fingers sneak into her shorts pocket to make contact with her birthday money, rolled tight as a candy cigarette. She feels proud. Alone like Dah. Looking out for her own self. No one knowing where she is. Dah would be glad to see her now: this is how he wants her to be.

———

The moon glowed like a coin in a blacksmith's forge. In the parking lot Twomey shook Mr. Crocker's enfolding soft hand,

and then held his breath behind a smile. The second the Wheels careened out of sight he exploded—jigging and twirling left-right-left on the spot with hands wagging up to that fog-defying moon. Faster. Nimble as the lad in Connaught, despite a few pounds. The Rumpelstiltskin of Saratoga Springs.

"I love you. I will never love anyone else."

He froze, just shy a heart attack. A moment later he believed he'd experienced the beginning of one. "Where are you?"

"Here. Inside. Waiting."

Twomey leaned to the open window of his own truck. "Shouldn't go slumming, love." Her body, her clothes, her perfume overfilled the cab. The truck was a Dodge, painted thickly white to discourage the rust that was nonetheless blooming again along every edge, like red lichen.

"I gave you everything a woman has to offer. Not good enough. Not what you wanted."

He did not want to join her inside the truck. But there were buildings, windows, all around. In a small town there's usually someone watching. So he squeezed in behind the wheel, shut the door quietly, depressing the latch. "I'll run you home. You're in no condition, Marianne."

"If I did something to myself—"

"What? Oh, for *God's* sake!"

"If I did you wouldn't care, would you? Wouldn't even miss me."

She was not drunk, he realized. He wished she were. The thickness in her speech came from the aftermath of long crying: mucus, congealed tears. "Come," he said. Made the effort to touch the back of her moon-bleached hand. "You're dead on your feet. I'll run you back."

"My husband hired a top lawyer. He's trying to cut me off. He wants custody of Devon! Why? What's he want her *for*? So I can't have her?"

Twomey had once asked her such questions, about Moi. And now he recalled the trip to Lake George after all, and times when Marianne brought both girls by the shed row, took them for ice creams, invited his Moira for sleep-overs any night business kept him late. That had been a good period in its way— though then, paying the shyster every cent he'd saved and mortgaging his future for the hope of keeping his Moi by him, safe from the Bitch-Pair—then, he'd thought himself a suffering Lazarus. But you can only *see* a time when you're carried beyond and it's frozen in the stream. And hadn't the bed part with Marianne been far beyond anything expected, a revelation to them both, back then when he believed in her charity so. It felt a century ago. Well and here he was, still. In one piece. He stroked her limp hand. "You'll get past it, love. You'll be all right."

"Like *you*, you mean? All right to find another fuck?"

Twomey *recognized* her: in him pity and disgust fused together. He jerked the key around in the ignition, and the Dodge convulsed as expected, rending the night with explosions and smoke. When Twomey turned sideways, finally satisfied with the sawing rhythm of the engine, the passenger door gaped open. She had gone.

———

Buenos, buenos, nodded the working lads as Twomey drove by other trainers' barns on the rutted path to his own four stalls,

and Twomey answered, "Morning!" And why, he asked himself, did they cling to the language of a place they prayed never
to be shunted back to?

A fine morning. The fog refreshed Twomey's sleep-starved
skin and eyes. The fog rolled and stretched like a live thing
between the shed-row barns and manure mounds, hot walkers,
and green-black clusters of tall trees stripped of lower branches
by generations of horses. The fog thickest by far out on the
training track. Nibbling a doughnut, Twomey slid from the
Dodge and stared a moment, trying to adjust. Hoofbeats pleas-
antly rattled the ground. "A wonder they don't have collisions in
this murk," he said aloud. The timekeeper's lookout tower, only
fifty yards away, was invisible. "Radar," said Twomey. Then the
fog parted, as if directed, to show Natty trotting up on Forry.
The gleam on the colt's hide as rich as the girl's satin jacket.

"Where were you goofing around all last night?" She
laughed, baring her excellent American teeth. She didn't care
about the answer.

Twomey shrugged, wiping crumbs off on his trousers.
"How's himself, this morning?"

"Kicking shit! I hardly could get the bridle on."

"Lovely." He gestured at the Dodge. "Care for a pastry?"

"That's breakfast, right? And probably an hour ago you
were still drinking vodka? You're so decadent. Maybe that's
the fascination. You're going to self-destruct, Twomey."

He felt soothed, almost flattered. "No, I won't. You're
here to save me."

"Hah! Is that what you really *think*?" The colt skittered
backward as if for emphasis. "By the way," she said, returning,
circling, "your crony's here. Over by the track." She nodded.
"Not that anyone can see—"

"My crony. Mr. Crocker?"

"Him. The Albanian. Ay-yup!" She trotted away, before he could ask where she'd heard that name.

The two men leaned on the rail. Nat cantered out on Forever You rockinghorse-easy. Before the starting position at the far long side they melted into fog. If only, Twomey prayed. If only the fog would lift *now*. It was all useless unless Mr. Crocker could *see* the object of his desire. Twomey wanted to see tears of avarice well in the other man's eyes. Thirty thousand, he'd begun by thinking, but the colt looked so brave, at his peak this fine morning, that he meant to hold out for the full thirty-five. Not a dime less. That should put Marianne happy again. A good price on Forever You would salve her pride as well as perk up both their bank accounts—and the sale would completely, naturally, end their connection. A good, clean break, but only *if* this fog . . . And yes, *yes,* the sky was growing more luminous and he could make out the shimmering blue mote of his rider's jacket, picking up speed.

"There! Can you see them?"

The tall man nodded. He'd tugged out his own big watch and tapped it just as Forry passed the quarter pole.

"She won't be pushing him hard," cautioned Twomey. Although to Nat he had murmured other orders.

"My God. Fifty seconds and change . . . He's *flying,*" whispered Mr. Crocker.

The gallop leveled out, flowing smooth as liquid. Three furlongs. Four furlongs. "Gee," said Mr. Crocker. He pressed the stop. There was a tremor in his hand.

"Well? Yes or no."

"What can I say, Irish? Man only lives once—" Crocker wiped a moist eye, then squinted, frowning. "What's the matter? Why's she jumping off him now? I hope nothing's wrong, is there? Christ, don't tell me he's *hurt?*"

Twomey stared, glued to the spot as his sweat-drenched colt was led off track, out a side gate. At each stride the foam-flecked head swung down low, a pendulum of pain. Beside him the girl walked with a pigeon-toed stiffness, as if she too were injured somewhere.

Mr. Crocker said, "This is awful. I can't stand here and watch this."

Twomey glanced up at him, and the look returned nearly made him flinch. He saw the lawyer's suspicion: that Twomey had set him up, had known of a lurking weakness in the colt and tried to unload him before the inevitable—

"Mr. Crocker, please now, don't be leaving!"

Nat came close. Nat was crying. Tears dribbled into mud on her wind-slapped cheeks. *I felt something give way in his left fore. I knew it was wrong. I didn't know what. . . .* Twomey knelt on the ground, hindered by his fat, to gently feel the colt's shins and ankles, cup them one by one softly as eggs, to gauge the temperature. The colt was unnaturally docile, in the pleading way of shocked animals that sense they need a human's help.

"Uh-uh. All deals are off." Mr. Crocker backed away. "In fact there's a certain lady I'm putting a phone call in to. What if that leg there is broken!"

"Please," said Twomey. "Stay until . . ." Cautiously he probed, hoping to discover the bulge of an easily reparable bowed tendon, but found none. A hairline crack, there might be. Possibly a bone chip off the knee? Need X rays to tell. The heat, and swelling, would emerge later. "Truth is, I'm feeling nothing here. This might be merely a minor setback, Mr. Crocker. A chance misstep! Nothing a bit more time won't fix, don't you see?"

Moi walks down to the wall that separates pavement from sand. She moves slowly. In Florida it's too hot to run; she's almost forgotten what running feels like. In a brown paper grocery bag she carries her whole collection of miniature horses. Newest are the chestnut mare and weanling. "Broodmare," "weanling." She knows words other kids don't. Her favorite half-hour is after supper, rearranging her collection on the windowsill of her room. When the trees are black but the sky still ballpoint-ink blue. She hums while setting up the band of horses in changing families and parades. Moi's mother wants never to see another horse again in her life. She doesn't often come into Moi's room.

For a while, belly-down on the beach, Moi builds race-tracks, paddocks, and ranches in the sand for her horses. Out across the bay the sun drops low, popsicle orange, then denser red. The sun sinks faster here than in the north. She scoops up all her horses back into the bag, and wades out in the quicksilver shallows. Under her feet the strong sand ribs are studded with fragments of shells. The salt water is warm as animals' breath. It's a long, long wade until the water laps up to her waist. This is what she feels like doing. Where the water tightens around her body she opens up the bag and shakes all her horses out, the stallions and mares and yearlings and weanlings, every last one, to see them tumbling alive and full of spirit beneath the surface until they glint down and away in a slight sea current.

About the Author

KAI MARISTED, born in Chicago, studied political science and economics in Munich and at MIT. She has worked as a broadcast journalist and playwright in Germany, as an international consultant, on teaching faculties in Europe and the United States, and in the racehorse world. The author of two novels, *Out After Dark* (1993) and *Fall* (1996), she lives on a farm near Boston with her two sons.

ABOUT THE TYPE

This book was set in Bembo, a typeface based on an old-style Roman face that was used for Cardinal Bembo's tract *De Aetna* in 1495. Bembo was cut by Francisco Griffo in the early sixteenth century. The Lanston Monotype Machine Company of Philadelphia brought the well-proportioned letter forms of Bembo to the United States in the 1930s.